The only way they could have taken him alive was to drug him

Lights came on everywhere and nearly blinded the unprepared Bolan. Before his eyes could adjust to the harsh glare, a hand came out of nowhere and slapped him hard across the face. The blow threatened to dislodge teeth and caused Bolan to bite the inside of his cheek. He tasted the immediate saltiness of his blood, smelled the ironlike scent, and as the sting of the slap wore down, he could sense the blood trickle down the side of his lip. There was little he could do about it. He tried to contain the blood, swallow it in pure stubbornness, but the angle of his head and body caused him to nearly choke on the thick puddle forming in his cheek.

Bolan spit out the blood and stared daggers at his captor. The man stood no higher than five and a half feet if he stood an inch. Shocks of unkempt black hair protruded from his head like stalagmites—it looked almost as if someone had glued it to his scalp in patches. He had a light complexion that stood out starkly against the dark hair and eyes. But his most prepossessing feature was his scent of destruction and death. Bolan knew the scent all too well and it practically emanated like a field of energy from this man.

Bolan felt the hot breath on his earlobe as the man spoke. "Every bad thing you experience is because of me…."

MACK BOLAN®
The Executioner

#272 Stealth Striker
#273 UForce
#274 Rogue Target
#275 Crossed Borders
#276 Leviathan
#277 Dirty Mission
#278 Triple Reverse
#279 Fire Wind
#280 Fear Rally
#281 Blood Stone
#282 Jungle Conflict
#283 Ring of Retaliation
#284 Devil's Army
#285 Final Strike
#286 Armageddon Exit
#287 Rogue Warrior
#288 Arctic Blast
#289 Vendetta Force
#290 Pursued
#291 Blood Trade
#292 Savage Game
#293 Death Merchants
#294 Scorpion Rising
#295 Hostile Alliance
#296 Nuclear Game
#297 Deadly Pursuit
#298 Final Play
#299 Dangerous Encounter
#300 Warrior's Requiem
#301 Blast Radius
#302 Shadow Search
#303 Sea of Terror
#304 Soviet Specter
#305 Point Position
#306 Mercy Mission
#307 Hard Pursuit
#308 Into the Fire
#309 Flames of Fury
#310 Killing Heat
#311 Night of the Knives
#312 Death Gamble
#313 Lockdown
#314 Lethal Payload
#315 Agent of Peril
#316 Poison Justice
#317 Hour of Judgment
#318 Code of Resistance
#319 Entry Point
#320 Exit Code
#321 Suicide Highway
#322 Time Bomb
#323 Soft Target
#324 Terminal Zone
#325 Edge of Hell
#326 Blood Tide
#327 Serpent's Lair
#328 Triangle of Terror
#329 Hostile Crossing
#330 Dual Action
#331 Assault Force
#332 Slaughter House
#333 Aftershock
#334 Jungle Justice
#335 Blood Vector
#336 Homeland Terror
#337 Tropic Blast
#338 Nuclear Reaction
#339 Deadly Contact
#340 Splinter Cell
#341 Rebel Force
#342 Double Play
#343 Border War
#344 Primal Law
#345 Orange Alert
#346 Vigilante Run
#347 Dragon's Den

The Don Pendleton's
Executioner®
DRAGON'S DEN

TORONTO • NEW YORK • LONDON
AMSTERDAM • PARIS • SYDNEY • HAMBURG
STOCKHOLM • ATHENS • TOKYO • MILAN
MADRID • WARSAW • BUDAPEST • AUCKLAND

First edition October 2007

ISBN-13: 978-0-373-64347-9
ISBN-10: 0-373-64347-0

Special thanks and acknowledgment to
Jon Guenther for his contribution to this work.

DRAGON'S DEN

Printed in U.S.A.

We succeed only as we identify in life, or in war, or in anything else, a single overriding objective, and make all other considerations bend to that one objective.

—Dwight D. Eisenhower

My objective is the freedom and security of America. I can't accept anything less and so all else, including my life, is a secondary consideration.

—Mack Bolan

Prologue

Washington Post, AP—Los Angeles

At approximately 7:15 a.m. PDT yesterday morning, narcotics officers of the L.A. County Sheriff's Department conducted a drug raid against a private yacht moored at the world-famous Marina del Rey. Sources report the yacht belonged to Raul Montavo, thirty-two, Hollywood's hottest Latin superstar. Police confiscated more than two hundred kilograms of opium and an undisclosed amount of heroin that one officer stated "was in plain view."

In a recent press conference, police spokesperson Martha Stellano said, "There were no fatalities or injuries during the raid. We found several bodies on board we believe are drug-related homicides."

When questioned about the identities of the deceased, police refused to comment until members of the immediate family were notified and causes of deaths determined. However, confidential sources indicate Raul Montavo is among those dead, as is the relative of a U.S. politician. There is no word yet on when police plan to provide further information.

Mack Bolan parked his rental car in the lot of the Los Angeles Sheriff's Department's Marina del Rey station and climbed from the air-conditioned interior into the midday August heat. The salty odor of the Pacific breezes stung his nostrils. Bolan pulled the mirrored sunglasses from his face and rubbed his eyes. He still felt the aftereffects of jet lag. Shortly after his return from a personal mission in Europe, Hal Brognola had called and begged him to go to California.

"What's up?" Bolan asked the Stony Man chief.

"We don't have all the facts quite yet, but it was enough to draw the Man's attention."

Mention of the President got Bolan's interest. "Let's back it up a little. Tell me what you know."

Brognola—head of the ultracovert Sensitive Operations Group, based at Stony Man Farm—told Bolan about the drug raid in Marina del Rey. Police had seized almost two hundred kilos of pure-grade opium. "And there were seven bodies," Brognola added.

"Any make on them?"

"Three were Asian, but local law enforcement is having one hell of a time putting names to faces."

"The other four?"

"Three Hollywood celebrities and Senator Simon Lipinski's daughter."

"Lipinski..." Bolan murmured. "From California?"

"Yes, the same Lipinski who's been making such a big stink over human rights on cheap, exported labor. He also happens to be a close personal friend of the President's family. Their kids went to high school together."

"That explains why the Man's involved."

"It gives us a possible reason for why someone might want to kill the girl, too," Brognola said. He paused and his tone softened. "She was just a college freshman, Striker. Barely out of high school with her whole life ahead of her, and just like that it's snuffed out."

Bolan could sense his friend's pain, even empathize with him, but he'd learned long ago he couldn't take those things personally. Vengeance, even exercised with righteous might, wasn't the sort of baggage a professional soldier could afford to carry—not that Bolan hadn't been tempted himself a time or three. He'd started his war against the Syndicate for the sake of vengeance but quickly converted it to a much higher call: duty.

"Lipinski may not be popular, but I doubt professionals would risk indiscriminate murder," Bolan replied. "If the killers wanted to send him a message, there are easier and more effective ways."

"We considered that possibility," Brognola said. "Truth be told, it's the drugs that concern us the most."

"Yeah, that's the angle I think we should play. Myanmar's the place I think of for that volume of pure opium."

"And they have the distribution network to back it up." Brognola's tone became matter-of-fact. "If anyone could move it without drawing attention, the heavies in the Golden Triangle would be *my* first choice."

"Practice makes perfect. There are two main transshipment points in that area. China, via the Thai route, or straight out of Myanmar. Myanmar still runs the major action, near as I recall. I'd say we start there," Bolan said.

"I'll make some calls to our DEA contacts, see what I can come up with as far as the current atmosphere. We'll make

the travel arrangements here. You can expect Jack there withi
the hour."

"So soon?" Bolan asked.

Brognola chuckled. "I already knew you'd say yes."

So four hours later the Executioner stood before th
LASD's station in jeans and a polo shirt. A DEA badge hun
from his belt, and the Beretta 93-R rode in a canvas shoulde
rig beneath his left arm.

Bolan entered the cool station, and a uniformed woma
behind the desk greeted him. Sergeant stripes adorned he
sleeve. She sported an enviable California tan, and her blon
hair was short. Her clear blue eyes immediately locked o
Bolan's pistol. He tapped the badge and the cop relaxed som

"Special Agent Cooper, DEA. I'm looking for Captai
Amherst."

"Do you have an appointment?" the young officer aske
him in a brisk, judicious tone.

"Not exactly, but I'm sure she's expecting me," Bola
replied. It didn't exactly constitute a direct answer to th
sergeant's question, but it wasn't entirely untrue, eithe
Bolan's experience in role camouflage had taught hi
middle-of-the-road tales always sounded the most believabl

"Maybe not, but just a moment," she replied, and reache
for a telephone.

Bolan turned to look out the glass doors and tuned out th
sergeant's conversation with whoever picked up at the oth
end. He couldn't have cared less about their internal burea
cracy. Bolan had come to find out about the death of an inn
cent college girl, and partly because his friend had asked f
his help.

"Captain Amherst will be with you in a moment, sir. Wou
you like something to drink while you wait?" the sergea
asked. Her voice had lost much of its edge; someone had o
viously instructed her to show him the first-class treatment

Bolan requested a mineral water. The sergeant smiled a

inclined her head, mumbled something, then turned to a compact refrigerator. She produced a plastic bottle a moment later and tossed it to him. He caught it one-handed and nodded his thanks.

Captain Amherst came around the corner of the hallway to Bolan's left. She strode with confidence, but the uniform didn't quite hide the curves of her slight, lean form. She wore her coal-black hair pulled back in a ponytail, but the oval face looked mature. She projected the air of a woman in charge, and Bolan immediately pegged her as a pro through and through. This wouldn't be easy.

"Captain Rhonda Amherst," she said, extending her hand.

"Matt Cooper," he replied.

"We weren't expecting anyone from the DEA just yet," she said.

"You probably weren't expecting us at all," Bolan said with a lopsided grin. "Or at least hoping."

She inclined her head slightly. "We're all in this together. Would you follow me, please?"

Bolan fell into step behind her. She led them to a conference room, flipped one of the wall switches and gestured toward a seat at the lit end of the long table. Amherst took the seat at the head of the table, folded her arms and leaned forward. She lowered her voice, but her eyes burned with pure scrutiny.

"Just to be sure I'm making no mistakes, I don't suppose you'd be willing to show me some *official* credentials?"

"No problem." Bolan reached into his back pocket and removed his wallet. He flipped out the identification, set it on the table in front of her and then added the badge to it.

She studied them a minute, then returned both to him. "Thanks. Can't be too careful these days."

"You'll find out they're in order when you call."

"Excuse me?"

"I saw your lips move," Bolan said. "You memorized the

ID number. I was letting you know I'll check out when you talk to the DEA."

Amherst couldn't do a thing about the sudden flush in her cheeks, and Bolan figured she knew it.

"So forget it," he said with a wave. "I'm not here to tread on toes, Captain. I'm only interested in tracing the origin of the drugs your people seized. Washington tells me it was high-grade opium, and there isn't too much of that flying around in the quantities we're talking here. You knew it would attract attention."

"I'm afraid it goes deeper than that, Agent Cooper."

"Tell me what you know," he said, leaning back and relaxing. Bolan figured she'd open up if he kept it loose. "Maybe I can help."

"Let me start by giving you some idea of our territory," she replied, getting out of her chair and walking over to a wall map. She stopped to eyeball him and added, "Only because it's important to our present circumstances. I won't try to snowball you."

Bolan nodded his acknowledgment.

"This map encompasses the entire jurisdiction of LASD. My particular area is that part shaded in light blue. Chiefly we provide service to the unincorporated parts of L.A. County broken into three main areas. Area Marina we monitor with six patrol boats, and we share responsibility with another division over at Santa Monica Bay. We're also responsible for a number of communities east of us and then of course Lost RD."

"The what?" Bolan interjected.

Amherst chuckled. "Our little pet name for a small island piece about a mile inland."

"You said this little tour you're giving me is important." Bolan shrugged. "In what way?"

"We recovered more opium in every one of our jurisdictional areas. This stuff has been located in everything from the mansions in Windsor Hills and Ladera Heights to the slums in View Park. That's what hasn't been in the papers. I'm under strict orders from the higher-ups to keep this as quiet as possible. I've argued with the sheriff. Hell, I even risked my rank by threatening to take it over his head and straight to the county commissioners, but he swore to me he's keeping them apprised. And yet, nada."

"So you don't believe him."

"I don't know what to believe anymore," she said with a deep sigh.

"Exactly how much opium are we talking about?" Bolan asked.

Amherst dropped into a chair next to the wall map. "Including the other night, I'd say we're up to about three thousand kilos. Frankly, it's more than we can handle. I'm actually *relieved* the DEA's involved. The sheriff has no choice now that the cat's out of the bag."

Most of what he'd just heard didn't make sense to Bolan. "So your superiors ordered you to keep it under wraps?"

"Until the other night. You know, it's a little easier to keep this quiet when the drugs aren't accompanied by seven corpses aboard a boat owned by one of the most famous actors in Hollywood."

"Raul Montavo?"

Amherst nodded and expressed distaste. "Yes, but I don't know why they called him the Latino Angel. I can testify he was anything but."

"Why's that?"

"The only reasons we even ran that raid was because of a reliable tip and a very friendly judge. Hell, he's probably one of the few judges on our side."

"You're too young to be that jaded," Bolan replied easily.

She frowned. "I got a lot on my plate, mister, believe me. There's more graft in the L.A. County court system than hookers on Hollywood Boulevard."

Bolan got to his feet. "I don't doubt you have a lot on your hands, so I'll keep out of your way and you keep out of mine. But you can bet I'll look into this further."

"That a promise or do you really mean it?" Amherst quipped.

"Funny," Bolan said. "You could help by keeping word of my involvement strictly need-to-know for now."

She did nothing to hide the derision in her tone as she threw up her hands. "Oh, great, another person who wants to keep this all hush-hush. Oh, well, who would I tell?"

"I don't want to keep it quiet because I have some hidden agenda," Bolan said in an even tone. "I just don't want to attract attention. If there are legit reasons the sheriff has kept a gag on this, fine. But if there's corruption involved, then it would be better if they didn't know anything about me until I can determine how deep it goes. Make sense?"

Amherst nodded. "Yes. And I owe you an apology, Cooper. I'm just tired, I guess. It seems like nobody wants to do anything about this."

"I do," Bolan said. "Trust me."

BOLAN SPOTTED THE TAIL in a nondescript sedan as soon as he left the parking lot of the LASD station. It didn't make sense. He hadn't been in-country even twelve hours, and nobody outside of Stony Man Farm would know of his existence or mission. That meant one of two things: Amherst had arranged for her people to follow him and see what he had up his sleeve, or someone already had the station under surveillance and Bolan's sudden arrival sparked their interest.

Bolan bet the latter scenario as the likeliest.

He'd use the next few minutes to decide if the followers were friend or foe. As Bolan merged with traffic on the interstate, he kept an eye on the tail through his rearview mirror and considered his options. Jack Grimaldi, Stony Man's ace pilot and longtime friend to Bolan, waited at the airport with the plane that had brought them there. Bolan had skipped renting a hotel room; he didn't figure they'd be long in L.A.

The Executioner didn't have a hotel, sure, but his tail probably didn't know that. The soldier quickly formulated his plan and then took the next exit when he spotted a hotel sign. Bolan kept to the outermost exit lane. His eyes flicked to the rearview in time to see the sedan slide into the lane next to his and keep back a couple of car-lengths. The maneuver left no doubt in Bolan's mind the followers weren't new to the game.

Bolan spotted the large hotel ahead of him and signaled early enough to make sure his tail saw where he planned to go. He swung into the parking lot and parked in one of the side-lot spaces. The L-shaped hotel was actually split into two sections separated by a breezeway at a right angle to the main office.

Bolan walked into the breezeway and broke into a jog after moving from view of the observers. He reached the other end, then turned right at the end. He followed this causeway to the rear of the hotel and crossed around the windowless back side of the office. Bolan waited about half a minute, then vaulted the eight-foot wall. He dropped to the pavement and skirted the wall to the edge of the lot.

Bolan peered around the wall and quickly spotted the sedan. The driver had pulled into the parking lot of a taco joint directly across from the hotel. It afforded them a virtually unobstructed view of the hotel. It seemed they meant no violent threat to the Executioner—at least not an immediate one—and Bolan planned to make sure it never got that far. He'd learned that sometimes discretion wasn't the better part of valor, and this was one of those times.

Bolan turned and strolled to the stoplight half a block away. He crossed with the light and then doubled back so he could approach from the rear. When he reached the building next to the taco stand, he circled it and came up on the sedan from the rear. He took the last twenty yards in a crouch and approached on the passenger side. Two men in crew cuts and short-sleeve shirts occupied the front seats. Bolan kept low and quietly tested the rear door handle. Locked.

Bolan went in hard.

He reached into the open window and grabbed the passenger by the collar. With his left hand, he shoved the man to the left and produced the Beretta 93-R in his right fist, pointing it toward the head of the driver.

"You packing?" he asked them.

The passenger yelped something as Bolan's rock-hard knuckles pressed against his neck, and the driver's eyes went wide. The men were young and inexperienced. They hadn't expected their quarry to become the aggressor, and Bolan had taken them by total surprise.

"I asked a question," Bolan said. "You guys packing?"

"Yeah, yeah," the driver replied.

"Right or southpaw?" Bolan asked him.

"Say what?"

"Are you right- or left-handed?"

"Right," he said. "Why?"

"You first, then. Use your left hand and dump the piece out the window."

"You're making a big mistake, asshole," the passenger finally squealed in outrage.

"So is he," Bolan said, gesturing in his partner's direction with the muzzle of the Beretta. He returned his attention to the driver. "Last chance. Lose the sidearm or it all ends here."

"Fine, fine," he said.

When Bolan heard the pistol hit the pavement outside, he ordered the passenger to carefully hand over his weapon. The guy complied. Bolan immediately recognized the Glock 21. He tucked the pistol at the small of his back, then commanded the pair to put their hands on the dash. He opened the rear door once they had done it and slid to the center of the backseat.

"Okay, let's have it," Bolan asked.

"You just stepped in a whole pile o' shit, pal," the passenger said. "You'll be at the top of Homeland Security's most-wanted list by close of business today."

"Somehow I don't think so," the Executioner replied.

"I don't get it," Hal Brognola said when Bolan related his en counter with the federal agents. "Why would this interest Home land Security? In fact, how would they even *know* about it?"

"No clue. But they admitted their orders were to pressur local authorities to keep this thing under wraps," Bolan replied "I kept my cover but it won't last. I'm sure they'll make calls I need them to back off this thing. I don't want to have to worr about friendlies getting caught in the cross fire if it goes hard."

Brognola sighed. "You got it. I'll make sure the order to stan down comes straight from the top. I'm sorry about this, Striker."

"Not your fault, Hal. This wasn't on my radar screen, either."

"So Captain Amherst told you they've seized three thou sand kilos of high-grade opium, huh?" Brognola recited "That's seriously heavy weight."

"Yeah, and it's obviously drawing more attention by th moment. That's why I need to move on this right now befor the entire area gets flooded with *real* DEA."

"If the press gets wind of this, DEA will be the least of you problems. All the major papers are carrying the yacht-rai story, and you know sooner or later someone's going to lea the rest of it. Reporters will swarm that town like nobody' business."

"Exactly," the Executioner replied. "And I'm not real bi on having my face splashed all over the six-o'clock news."

"You have a plan?"

"It's sketchy, but it's all I have to go on. Amherst told me about the other surrounding towns within her jurisdiction where they also seized large quantities of the same purity. One of them is Ladera Heights. According to my LAPD contacts, the Bloods control all major drug action in this area. I need to know who's in charge."

"I'll put Bear to work. You'll have it within the hour."

Bolan believed him. Aaron "the Bear" Kurtzman wore his nickname well. Not only because of his wrestlerlike body, but also because of the heart to match. The leader of Stony Man's crack cybernetics team seemed serious, but he hadn't permitted the internal man to mirror that gruff exterior. That sensitivity set him apart from most men who'd experienced the kind of trauma he had—confined to a wheelchair by a bullet in the spine—and Bolan considered Kurtzman to be one of the most intelligent people in the world.

"You can send it through the plane's uplink," Bolan said. "I'll be waiting there with Jack. Out here."

Bolan broke the connection, then took the exit ramp leading to LAX and the private hangar leased under one of Stony Man's paper companies. While the ultracovert group operated at the pleasure of the President, its actions weren't consistent with constitutional law. Some of Stony Man's past operations inside the territorial borders of the U.S. would have been considered by most as highly illegal, even with the leeway granted to federal agencies investigating terrorism. That's why Brognola insisted on the provision of cover names and federal-agency credentials, as much to reduce Stony Man's culpability as to protect the identities of its operatives.

The Executioner didn't really need the forged documents, since he could get what he wanted by other means. He disliked working with allies—the other team members of Stony Man notwithstanding—and what he couldn't glean from his many intelligence contacts or free access to Stony Man's databases, he could get through enemy interrogation. Bolan rarely had to implement the latter solution and he didn't believe in torture, chemical or otherwise, although he occasionally understood the need for such methods.

Bolan reached the airport in fifteen minutes. He pulled his rental car around the rear of the hangar—the section not visible from the tarmac—and then strolled inside. In the center of the hangar sat a converted Gulfstream C-20 jet. At just over eighty feet in length, it sported a pair of Rolls-Royce Spey engines and had a range of more than thirty-six hundred nautical miles. Any casual observers wouldn't have noticed anything out of the ordinary until they looked inside. Bolan had become quite familiar with the decor, which included state-of-the-art surveillance, countersurveillance and secure communications equipment. A weapons locker took up the rear of the plane and contained the latest gadgets. John "Cowboy" Kissinger, Stony Man's resident weapon smith, had stocked it with enough firepower to start a small war. Nothing unusual for the man they called the Executioner.

"What say ye, Sarge?" Grimaldi asked, looking up briefly from an air chart. He'd never dropped the moniker, a reference to Bolan's early days as a sniper sergeant in the U.S. Army.

"We'll be sticking around for a bit longer," Bolan said as he took a seat at the table across from Grimaldi.

The pilot nodded, then stabbed a finger in the direction of a small stainless steel carafe. "There's some java if you're interested."

Bolan shook his head. "Not really attractive in this heat. What are you doing?"

"Looking over some charts," Grimaldi said. "I got talk from Hal we might end up going out of country. There was some mention about the sunny beaches of the Golden Triangle, perhaps?"

"Yeah. You know, I've been meaning to ask you, most of your navigation is done solely by computers these days. Why do you still use paper charts?"

"Computers fail, navigation systems go out and GPS units have been known to land pilots in Alaska who *were* going to Hawaii. I'm all about a backup plan, Sarge."

"Far be it for me to interfere with a master at work," Bolan said with a chuckle.

The soldier rose and went to the reinforced doors of the weapons locker in the aft compartment. He punched in a nine-character alphanumeric code on a keypad attached to the heavy steel and the latch came free. The weapons reflected the dim blue lights recessed in the sides and top of the cabinet with an oily gleam. The complement included an M-16 A-4/M-203 combo, M-4 5.56 mm carbine and one FN FNC submachine gun. The armory also held a SIG-Sauer SSG 3000 sniper rifle, a spare Beretta 93-R with twin clips and a dozen Diehl DM-51 grenades. Finally, Bolan's eyes rested briefly on the .44 Magnum Desert Eagle. This gas-operated hand cannon utilized a rotating bolt system and fired 300-grain rounds at a muzzle velocity just shy of 1,500 feet per second.

Bolan picked the Beretta and FN FNC for this trip, as well as a few DM-51 grenades. He'd be entering gangland territory, which meant some autofire and a few low-yield antipersonnel grenades might come in handy, but heavy assault weapons probably wouldn't be necessary. In fact, he didn't even know if he had a target yet. He could only hope Stony Man's intelligence would point him in the right direction.

After drawing his selections, Bolan secured the armory doors, then left the plane with his utility bag. He crossed the hangar to the living quarters, where he found a shower. He stripped, turned on the hot water and enjoyed the high-pressure spray, washing away the grime and dirt of the day. He then turned the nozzle to allow about two minutes of icy spray to cool his body. Bolan finished showering, toweled dry and then donned his skintight blacksuit and slid his feet into a pair of combat boots with vulcanized neoprene soles. He then returned to the plane.

Grimaldi jerked his thumb at a computer terminal set into the two-seater communications panel against the starboard side. "Your transmission from Bear just arrived."

Bolan nodded and took a seat at the computer terminal. He punched in his access code, and the information immediately displayed across two separate LCD screens. One screen rendered photographs and dossiers taken from LASD evidence computers, with detailed reports of every raid where they had recovered drugs matching the parameters Stony Man already had. Bolan shook his head, unable to resist grinning at Kurtzman's ability to hack straight into any computer network to get the intelligence Bolan needed. The Executioner scanned the information, which basically confirmed what Amherst had said.

"Well, at least Amherst is telling the truth," Bolan said aloud.

"What's that?" Grimaldi asked.

"This Rhonda Amherst," Bolan replied. "She's the Marina del Rey station chief with LASD. It looks like she gave me the straight story."

Grimaldi just hummed an acknowledgment as Bolan turned his attention to the second screen. He tapped the paging key and quickly identified the key information he'd been looking for. Records from the Gang Support Section of the LAPD currently listed Lavon Hayes as the leader of the Bloods, but his current whereabouts were unknown. The file gave too many possible locations, so Bolan mentally filed the information for future reference and pressed on. And then the Executioner got a hit. The GSS briefs listed Antoine Pratt as being Hayes's second-in-command. Already Pratt had spent the better part of his life in juvenile for everything from petty theft to drug possession, and he currently had a half-dozen warrants pending for additional crimes.

A real pillar of the community, Bolan thought. "Looks like this intel from Bear might pan out," he said as he stored the downloaded intelligence and put the computer into hibernation. He went to where he'd stashed his equipment and geared up.

"Where you going?"

"It's time to find out who was supposed to be on the receiving end of these shipments."

"Going to knock on some doors, are you?" Grimaldi asked with a knowing wink.

"More like kick them down," the Executioner replied.

MACK BOLAN PLACED his first kick in the most literal sense.

The soldier put his foot against the front door of Antoine Pratt's two-story flat in Ladera Heights. He stood out like a specter, his blacksuit stark against the cream-colored walls illuminated by mood lights. Mostly warm earth tones set off the decor, which looked more luxurious than its run-down exterior. Pratt had probably tried to keep up appearances with the other houses along the block so his didn't stand out in any way. Bolan swept the area with the muzzle of his FNC and locked on viable targets almost immediately.

A pair of house guards in flannel shirts and bandanas came out of their loungers in the living room and reached for pistols tucked in their waistbands. Neither of the young men seemed to care Bolan already had them dead to rights.

Bolan squeezed the trigger and the FNC chugged in his hands. He couldn't miss at that range. The hail of 5.56 mm NATO slugs stitched a path across their bellies, tearing through vital organs and sending blood spray in every direction. They twisted inward and collided with each other before dying on their feet. Their corpses hit the carpeted floor with dull thuds.

The Executioner bounded up the flight of steps to his right after clearing his six. He reached the top of the steps and immediately went prone on the upper landing when he caught motion in his periphery. Two more gangbangers opened up on him with pistols. One had enough sense to stay behind the cover of an archway, but the other practically strutted toward Bolan, his pistol held high and sideways as he triggered round after round. The warrior rolled over once, came to his knee and triggered a corkscrew burst. High-velocity slugs riddled the hoodlum's body and knocked him off his feet. The dead youth's partner popped off a few more hasty rounds before ducking behind the archway.

Bolan detached a Diehl DM-51 from his load-bearing harness. The German-made hand grenade had proved one of the most effective tools of Bolan's trade. The hexagonal shape of the grenade body contained more than six thousand 2 mm steel balls packed into a PETN high explosive, making it a superbly effective offensive blast device. When requiring defensive capabilities, the Executioner could attach a plastic sleeve to the grenade with a simple half-twist locking motion, thereby causing a shower of superheated steel fragments to disperse in every direction for antipersonnel effects.

Bolan attached the sleeve, yanked the pin and threw himself into a closed door to get out of the hallway. The warrior didn't see the grenade explode but he felt it; the resulting screams from his opponent told the rest of the tale. Bolan sensed a presence behind him and spun as he dropped to one knee, finger poised on the FNC trigger. A woman cloaked only in a skimpy towel emerged from a door in the wake of steam clouds and shrieked at the sight of him.

Bolan shook his head, got to his feet and jerked a thumb in the direction of the bathroom. "Back inside."

She didn't argue with him.

Bolan stepped into the hallway and advanced along it. He could sense the quarry somewhere ahead; his instincts had taken over the moment he entered the house. He could almost smell the fear on his enemy. Pratt had no intention of running. If anything, Bolan suspected the guy would make a stand right here on his own turf, even if it might kill him, and that made it doubly important Bolan take him alive. Pratt remained the only one who could tell the Executioner why so much dope had been funneled into Los Angeles over the past couple of months.

Bolan began a room-to-room sweep, the FNC ready, but met no further resistance. He also didn't find Antoine Pratt. After completing his search, Bolan headed for the stairs. He made it halfway down before the front door burst wide-open and a trio of hoods in gang colors came through the door followed by a fourth who matched the photo of Pratt in Bolan's intelligence from Stony Man. Two of the gangbangers had their hands full with cases of beer.

All four wore the same expression of surprise upon seeing the Executioner, but none of them were ready to deal with the threat. Bolan leveled the FNC in their direction and neatly shot holes through the cases of beer they carried. The man walking next to Pratt—who obviously acted as bodyguard to the Bloods lieutenant—seemed to be the only one prepared for action as he reached beneath the loose T-shirt he wore and produced a semiautomatic pistol.

Bolan triggered a 3-round burst that blew the man's skull apart and showered his companions with gray matter.

The remaining three black youths froze in place.

"Grab the floor!" Bolan ordered the trio.

They immediately dropped what remained of their brews and did as ordered. Bolan continued down the steps and relieved them of their pistols before securing their hands behind them with plastic riot cuffs. That done, Bolan hauled Pratt to his feet and tossed him face-first against a nearby wall. He placed the hot muzzle of the FNC at the base of Pratt's skull.

"What are you, the feds?" Pratt asked. He made a good attempt to hide the fear in his eyes, but it didn't fool Bolan for a moment. "I want a lawyer."

"Shut up, Pratt," Bolan said. "Here's how this goes. I ask questions and you give me answers. If I even think you're lying, I kill you. Simple enough?"

Pratt just nodded, the hatred evident in his features. Bolan didn't give a damn right at the moment. He would have taken the opportunity to clean out the Bloods altogether had he not felt it would detract from his mission. The key here would be to get to the source of the opium imports. Then, and only then, would he be able to shut down the pipeline. The Bloods couldn't profit from the supply if he neutralized the supplier.

"Word has it you're running this outfit with Lavon Hayes out of the picture," Bolan said. "I know you're on the receiving end of this recent influx of drugs. Tell me who's supplying it."

"I don't know what the fuck you're talking about," Pratt sputtered. "We haven't seen a dime of that stuff, which means somebody's going to end up dead because they're cutting into our territory."

"The only one that'll wind up dead is you if I don't get a better answer." Bolan's tone implied the validity of the threat.

"Then I'm dead, whitey, because I don't got no answers. Whoever's running this stuff through here had better watch their ass. L.A. belongs to the Bloods."

"L.A. belongs to law-abiding citizens," Bolan said. "So here's a new slogan for your graffiti artists—stay out of my way and end this business. Otherwise I'm going to come back here and punch your ticket. Get it?"

"I thought you was going to kill me."

Bolan's cold and friendless smile matched the tone in his voice. "Not today."

"You leave me alive, you won't be long for this life."

"Yeah, sure," Bolan said. "If I hear you're still in operation a week from now, it'll be *you* who's not long for this life."

Bolan grabbed the drug-dealing gang member by his collar once more and took him to the floor. He then turned and left through the front door. He reached the rental he'd left parked a half block away within a minute and soon reached the expressway.

The probe hadn't revealed much in the way of viable information, but Bolan now believed these drugs had nothing to do with the Bloods. He'd taken the mere chance that a grasp at straws might lead him somewhere; instead, he'd come away with more questions than answers. The Executioner had been in L.A. six hours, and he still didn't know where the opium had come from or why somebody would have wasted seven people over a couple hundred kilos, especially when they had already managed to get twenty times that inside the country in the past sixty days. Bolan hoped Stony Man's far-reaching network came up with something more solid.

In the meantime, he still had a couple more doors on his list.

Even from early childhood, Rhonda Amherst knew she wanted to be a police officer.

She didn't necessarily believe in destiny, but she felt something like that every time she thought of her inevitable entry into law enforcement. On her twelfth birthday she'd become copresident of the Neighborhood Watch Program of suburban L.A., and by fifteen she had joined the Sheriff's Explorer Program. By eighteen she'd been accepted to UCLA under a scholarship, and during her years in college she served with the Big Sister program. Amherst graduated UCLA with honors at age twenty-two holding a degree in criminal justice.

That's when life really began for Amherst. She went straight into the Los Angeles Sheriff's Recruit Training Center, graduated top of her class, and soon she returned to patrol the same streets of the neighborhood where she had grown up. Amherst volunteered for every special assignment or training course she could manage when they came along—few and far between as they were—but it eventually paid off and got her the notice of the entire LASD and eventually led to her promotion to sergeant. One of her favorite volunteer jobs involved boat patrols done in extra shifts. From a very early age she had taken to the water like a bird dog. Before she knew it, her CO recommended Sergeant Amherst for a position as his lieutenant when he took the captaincy at Marina del Rey Station. Four short years later, he suffered a stroke that disabled him permanently, and since Amherst happened to be testing for a captain's slot, she seemed a shoo-in for the position. She had just completed her second year as captain, not only one of the youngest captains in the department but also the first female to achieve that rank so quickly.

What had gained Rhonda Amherst the most respect in her position was that she'd accomplished everything through hard work. She didn't subscribe to the political maneuvering that involved others. Most of her subordinates and fellow officers would have described her as easygoing and friendly, a leader's leader who really cared about each and every officer under her command, but also as a tough and no-nonsense cop. She held a second-degree black belt in tae kwon do, and possessed an unrivaled record of felony arrests.

All of her success came from the internal drive to protect others with integrity and honor. That same drive caused her to put down the bottle of scented bath crystals she had just started to pour into her garden tub and go answer the jangling telephone. She'd heard a little activity over the scanner but chose to ignore it as it didn't sound like anything going down in her district. Beside the fact, she tried to reserve at least one night a week where she didn't think about work, time she chose to devote to herself.

"Yes?" she said into the receiver.

"It's me."

"Nesto, to what do I owe such a pleasure?" Amherst teased him. "I haven't heard from you in weeks. You don't call, you don't write—"

"This is more of an official call, I'm afraid."

Amherst had known Nesto Lareza since high school. They were just about as best friends as a man and woman could be next to taking it to the romantic level, which they had once tried in an exercise that failed miserably. Amherst could hear the tone in Lareza's voice, and he didn't sound happy.

"What's going on?"

"I'm here at the house of Antoine Pratt," Lareza said. "Got

called here after someone dialed 9-1-1 and reported shot fired and what sounded like an explosion."

"Pratt lives in Ladera Heights," she said, recalling it almos instantaneously from her memory. She'd made it a habit to be familiar with the movements of certain elements. "Did some-body finally take him out? Another rival gang or something? If so, I'm throwing a party."

"This wasn't a rival gang," he said. "Just one guy."

Amherst felt her blood immediately run cold. She couldn't explain why, but for some reason Lareza's statement made her think of Matt Cooper. Amherst had called to check Agen Cooper's credentials as soon as he left, and the Departmen of Justice confirmed not only his status with the DEA but his authorization to investigate the sudden flood of drugs into Los Angeles. And further, people at the "highest level would ap-preciate it if Captain Amherst cooperated with Cooper's in-vestigation in every way possible."

Amherst tried to keep her voice neutral. "So why call me?"

"Well, Pratt's not talking but one of his boys got diarrhea of the mouth as soon as we arrived. This guy had some inter-esting things to tell me, but I don't want to get into any more of that over the phone. I think we should meet."

"You told me this was more official."

Lareza sighed deeply. "Look, it *is* official but it's also kind of unofficial, what I have to tell you. Can you just meet me Rhonda?"

"Sure," she said. "Tell me where and when."

"You remember Cappie's?"

"Of course," she said, recalling the renovated fishing whar turned restaurant that had become a popular hangout fo UCLA alumni.

"I get off at eleven, so I'll meet you there about quarter-to-twelve. Okay?"

"I'll be there," she said, and hung up.

It had been one of the weirdest calls she could ever remem

ber receiving from Lareza, but also one of the most intriguing. She couldn't fathom why whatever had transpired at the home of Antoine Pratt would have anything to do with her. Apparently Lareza felt otherwise, and she'd learned to trust her friend's judgment. Something Lareza heard obviously led him to believe it would be of interest to Amherst, and yet sensitive enough he didn't want to draw undue attention.

Amherst could only recall confiding in him recently on one topic, and that had been the sheriff's unwillingness to pursue the major influx of opium into L.A. County neighborhoods. Now, with the DEA involved, it only stood to reason the stuff would start going public and the need for secrecy made naught. But on the other hand, maybe the sheriff's position hadn't changed. Maybe more existed here than Amherst believed, and maybe this involved more than just drugs and gangs.

Amherst would have to keep her wits about her, because in a very short time she knew she'd need to call on them under the direst circumstances.

THE FISH BATTER and din of voices were the only two things thicker than the smoke in Cappie's Lounge.

An observer might have concluded the lounge catered mostly to the yuppie clientele, but, in fact, Cappie's served a mixer of rowdy college students—mostly they congregated in the bar and pool area.

The alumni or faculty—the adults, in other words—confined their activities to the restaurant. In either case, Amherst had come to adore the lounge. For one thing, most cops wouldn't be caught dead in such a place, except in an undercover role. That meant it unlikely anybody would spy on her there or she'd run into anyone uncomfortable.

Lareza studied Amherst over the rim of his glass. He'd been watching her intently as she devoured her third helping of fish. He seemed almost stone-faced except for that damn smirk that occasionally played across his lips. The fact Amherst couldn't figure out why he kept staring at her with that ridiculous expression only served to irritate her. Finally, Amherst put down her fork, wiped away the grease from her lips and washed her food down with a swig from an ice-cold bottle of beer.

"I hate to eat alone," she said. "Why didn't you order anything?"

"I told you I'm not hungry."

Amherst dropped her napkin on the table next to her plate, grabbed the bottle in one hand, stuffed the other in her pocket and then leaned back. She wiped the bottle across her forehead. The temperature seemed to have gone up ten degrees since they arrived forty minutes earlier.

"So, what was so damn hush-hush you couldn't tell me on the phone?"

Lareza sat forward and put both forearms flat on the table. His hands visibly tightened as he dropped his tone some, making it much more difficult to hear him over the music blaring from the jukebox speakers mounted strategically throughout the establishment. His dark brown eyes gleamed under the diffuser-shade lamp that hung over their table. He'd always been a handsome guy, partly rugged with his dark skin and partly teddy bear with those dimples. He wore his black hair short and slicked back.

"The guy I questioned tonight, he's a bodyguard and enforcer for Antoine Pratt."

"You already mentioned that," Amherst replied with a nod. "What's his story?"

"His story is this mystery perp scared the living shit out of him. Said the guy was a big son of a bitch, dressed up like some type of commando. Apparently he just walked in and started shooting the place up and blowing it all to hell. Preliminary evidence says there were automatic weapons and high explosives used in Pratt's house. Crime scene thinks possibly grenades."

"And you believed him?" Amherst asked as she cocked one eyebrow.

"Hell, yeah, I believed him!" Lareza noticed her look around and lowered his voice self-consciously. "Sorry."

Amherst could already see where this conversation would end up, but she couldn't ignore what Lareza had just revealed. "Automatic weapons aren't anything new here. But military-grade explosives, that sounds a bit more serious."

"You're goddamn right it is," Lareza said. "And I'll tell you something else. This wasn't done in gangland style one bit. This guy hit the place like a professional all the way."

"What did he look like?"

"Tall with dark hair. Pratt's guy couldn't really get a look at his face because I guess he had it smeared with shoe polish or something, but he remembered the guy's eyes were blue because they stood out so much. Said he'd never seen colder eyes on someone than this bastard."

Amherst could feel that sensation go through her again, like ice pulsing in her veins. Other than the commando outfit and face paint, the guy matched Matt Cooper's description perfectly: big, dark hair and some very intense blue eyes. Yes, she couldn't deny that sounded exactly like Cooper, and moreover she couldn't deny how betrayed she felt. At that moment, she had an even bigger problem. While she'd known Lareza for a lot of years she didn't entirely trust him. In the past he *had* kept her other secrets, though, and if she needed a friend now was the time.

"That guy sounds like a dead ringer for a man who came to my office late this afternoon."

Something changed in Lareza's expression. "What man?"

"Well, I wasn't supposed to tell anybody, but you know how to keep your mouth shut. You can't breathe a word of it to anybody, Nesto, I'm telling you straight."

"I swear, I won't say nothing," Lareza replied, crossing himself and kissing the crucifix hanging from his neck. "But what the hell are you being so damn secretive about?"

"Because I don't know where any of this is going yet, and

I don't want anyone jumping to conclusions and doing something stupid."

"It would be a little hard to do something stupid when I don't even know what the hell you're talking about."

"This guy who came to see me, his name is Matt Cooper. He's an agent with the DEA…or so he claims."

"The feds? Why would they be so interested in any of this? It's a local problem."

"Because of the volume of drugs that have come into the greater Los Angeles area in just the past three months." Amherst looked around, took a swig of beer and continued, "There's been a lot more than you know about, Nesto. A *lot* more. I'm talking major weight, not just a few hundred kilos being pushed around."

"Great. So how come I don't know anything about this?" Lareza asked.

"For the same reason you didn't know about any of the other stuff I've told you about," she said. "The sheriff and city politicians have been trying to keep it quiet. They didn't just threaten my job, like I told you before. They threatened to go to a judge and get a gag order."

"Why didn't they?"

Amherst shrugged and said, "I managed to convince them I'd remain silent, I guess."

"Except for what you've told me," Lareza replied. He cracked a smile.

She smiled and nodded. "Except for what I told you, yes."

"So let me get this straight. There's been major drugs recovered at a number of key locations in the past few months, and now all of the sudden you get paid a visit from the DEA."

"Right," she said, "and I got in touch with some friends in Washington about this Cooper, just to be sure it wasn't some kind of trap. Maybe put there by the sheriff to spy on me."

"You figure if he's legitimate he wouldn't prefer you keep quiet. He'd want you to make some noise."

"Maybe," she said. "But if the guy your gangbanger describes is Cooper, then there might be another way to look at this."

"How's that?"

"Maybe Cooper's DEA, maybe he isn't," she said. "I'd guess he's some sort of special operator in town to rattle cages. He figures it's probably one of the local gangs trying to get the corner on the market here in L.A., or maybe even a rival faction."

"So he shakes some trees to see who falls out," Lareza concluded. "And he doesn't want you to tell your higher-ups in case they're involved somehow."

"Or maybe he just doesn't want local interference. He might have his own leads to follow. Hell, Cooper might not even be interested in the drugs at all. This could be about something else entirely. He did tell me he wasn't here to step on our toes."

"Oh, bullshit! They always say that, Rhonda."

"I don't know, maybe you're right. But I swear to you, Nesto, there was just something different about this guy. Don't ask me to explain it. I can't. I just know—" she stopped and chewed her lip a moment "—I just know he's not like most other men."

Lareza expressed surprise. "Get serious! You're starting to sound like you've fallen head-over-heels for this Cooper."

That caused her to laugh. "Don't be ridiculous. I just have this sense about him. It's only a feeling, but I get the notion he's really a good man."

"Well, good man or not, he just blew peace between the gangs wide-open, and that only stands to make more trouble." Lareza wagged his finger at her almost as if reminding her of another time, a time back during the gang riots following the announcement that vindicated several police officers charged with nearly beating to death a black man.

Amherst waved away the notion. "This situation is entirely different, and you know it. There will never be peace between these gangs. Especially if drugs continue to flood the market at the current rate."

"Seems to me this is about way more than drugs," Lareza said, sitting back and folding his arms in resolve.

Amherst cocked her head. "What do you mean?"

"You just said it yourself," Lareza said. "Let's suppose this Cooper's a real federal cop, or even some kind of special troubleshooter."

The concept intrigued Amherst. "You mean, special ops."

"Right. It's no secret every federal agency in this country was required to lend resources when the administration formed Homeland Security. They all work together now. Task forces and suchlike are very common."

"I might agree there was something to what you were saying. But then that leaves me with one question where Cooper's concerned. How come he came alone?"

"You don't know for a fact he's operating alone," Lareza replied in a matter-of-fact tone. "Maybe that's what he wanted you to think."

Amherst certainly couldn't deny the possibility, so she chose to keep any further thoughts about Cooper to herself and turned the conversation to other things. They made small talk for a while, bantered a few war stories and discussed the latest gossip within the department.

The digital clock read 1:42 a.m. by the time Amherst climbed behind the wheel and started for home. The quiet caused her mind to wander some, and her head ached with the echoes of nearly two hours of continuous loud music and having to shout now and again to be heard.

As she continued toward home her thoughts turned toward Cooper. Why couldn't she get the guy out of her head? For the first time in a while she found herself unsure of what to do next. She supposed she could issue a BOLO, but if he found out she had people looking for him he might get spooked. Then again he didn't really have any reason to run anywhere if he was legit.

The sudden squawks of activity over a dash-mounted scanner demanded her attention. She listened carefully for what lay behind the general tones of panic underlying the radio traffic. Something major had just gone down over on Lincoln Boulevard, a few blocks from Fox Hills Mall in Culver City.

Amherst knew immediately what it meant. Whoever had taken the heat to Pratt had just unleashed some more on the smaller Hispanic gangs neighboring Ladera Heights—gangs that had close ties to the fabled La Eme.

Amherst turned her SUV around and headed straight for Lincoln Boulevard.

Mack Bolan had never intended to bring war to the gangs of Los Angeles.

Kurtzman's intelligence had pointed to gang activities in Culver City, and after Bolan's investigation of Antoine Pratt didn't reveal much, the Executioner opted to look elsewhere for his answers. The enemies Bolan now faced were clearly members of the Thirteenth Street Gang, an up-and-coming group with purported ties to the famous La Eme. An acronym for La Muerta, La Eme had grown into the largest Hispanic prison gang in the country with outside connections to Hispanic gangs in major cities like Los Angeles, Miami and Chicago.

It stood to reason only a major gang could coordinate such mass shipments of opium into the country, but so far Bolan's intelligence hadn't pointed to any specific gang. The slaughter of those on the yacht coupled with the reluctant attitude of leaders high in the ranks of local government, told Bolan the shippers were getting major cooperation. Most of the gangs in L.A. depended on violence and intimidation, and of late Americans had not taken lightly to the general attitude that law-abiding citizens were just a pushover. It hadn't worked for terrorists and it wouldn't work for gangs.

The battle had been joined just minutes after Bolan left the tavern hangout of Javier Nuñez, the number-one guy inside the Thirteenth Street Gang who used the local watering hole as a base of operations. Bolan had solicited no more cooperation from Nuñez than he had from Pratt, and in this case the gang leader had the extra muscle to back his claims on most of the Culver City territory. Not that it mattered. Bolan didn't recognize Nuñez's reign over Culver City any more than he recognized Pratt's over Ladera Heights. Los Angeles belonged to its law-abiding citizens, and if Bolan had to take a brief timeout from his mission to teach that lesson to Nuñez, then that was just the hand he'd been dealt and he'd play it any way he could.

At the moment, however, the numbers were running off in his head. He'd been in town for six hours now, and come no closer to discovering the source of the drugs flooding the market. All he'd encountered so far were thugs bent on murder and destruction. But his trip hadn't been entirely for naught. He'd come to an assured conclusion the L.A. gangs were not behind the drug shipments.

Nuñez's crew had followed Bolan out of their home neighborhood, and then a chase ensued down Lincoln Boulevard before eventually terminating in the parking lot of a major mall. Bolan had learned a few things in his years of soldiering experience. One of those lessons involved securing a strategic holding position when preparing to launch an assault against an enemy of superior numbers.

Tonight had proved no exception.

From the limited cover of his vehicle, the Executioner swung the FN FNC into target acquisition on one of his gangland targets and squeezed the trigger. The weapon chattered as a flurry of 5.56 mm NATO rounds zipped through the young banger's chest and ripped exit holes in his back. The youth left his feet and his body slammed into the Lincoln "ghetto-cruiser" behind him. This impact broke the side mirror of the black, flashy Lincoln, and he left a gory streak on the window.

Bolan turned to his next target, a hood with a teardrop tattoo and twin pistols clutched in his fists. The warrior grimaced a moment as the kid didn't look more than sixteen or seventeen. It was hardly Bolan's preference to shoot teenagers and misguided youths, but he also knew the gang member knew right from wrong and had chosen a path. And whether the Executioner liked it or not, the gleaming .45-caliber semiautomatics clutched in his fist were real, and Bolan had to assume they were loaded with real bullets. Bolan triggered a second short burst from the FNC. The rounds cut a deep swathe in the gangbanger's gut and dropped him to the pavement.

Another gangland cruiser pulled up and Bolan decided to go EVA. He'd parked his car in a strategic position in the dark, deserted parking lot of the mall, which would give him the angling room he needed to deal with this new threat. The thudding in his ears of exertion drowned out the sounds of his boots slapping the serpentine sidewalk that wound through the exterior landscape of the mall. Bolan could barely make out the sounds of pursuit.

To the casual observer it would have appeared the quartet of gang members that bailed from the second vehicle were chasing down their quarry, but, in fact, Bolan had a plan. He would draw them into an ambush and turn the tables on them when they least expected it. Bolan quickly located a point near the main entrance doors of the mall that would provide adequate cover but take his pursuers by surprise. He didn't have to wait long. The foursome rounded the corner, and Bolan let loose with the FNC.

The first one to fall took two full bursts, one in the stomach and the other in the chest. The high-velocity rounds threw him into the gangbanger at his heels and the two violently thrashed about. The other pair began to run in circles, the shock and unbelief apparent on their faces, which glowed with ghostly pallor even in the poor lighting from faraway streetlights. Bolan caught the pair with a controlled, sustained firestorm from the FNC. The two gang members twisted and screamed with the repeated impact of slugs in tender flesh.

Bolan dropped the nearly spent magazine from its well and

loaded a fresh one. He put the FNC in battery and heard the scuffle of feet behind him. The warrior dropped as he turned and swung the muzzle of his assault rifle to deal with any threat. Bolan's eyes tracked to the source of the noise as he started to squeeze the trigger. He let off just in time to keep from gunning down Captain Rhonda Amherst.

"What the hell are *you* doing here?" she demanded.

Bolan noticed she hadn't lowered her pistol so he didn't let the FNC waver. "I could ask you the same question."

"I'm responding to a call." She cocked her head. "Are you the call?"

"Probably," he replied in a grim tone.

She gave a curt nod and finally lowered her sidearm. "I think we better talk."

"Sure, but right now my hands are full."

She shook her head and jabbed her thumb in the direction of her SUV. "I have a scanner. There won't be any more trouble. Two of our units just stopped a car headed this way filled with Thirteenth Street Gang reinforcements."

Bolan lowered his own weapon now. "Fine. My car's back there."

"Leave it. This place will crawl with both my people and LAPD in less than a minute."

"So what?"

"They're going to have questions. You want to be around here to answer them? I don't. And I sure as hell can't keep you being here quiet if you're going to draw this much attention to yourself."

Bolan got to his feet. "It wasn't by design."

"Maybe not, but it is what it is."

He couldn't argue with her logic. Bolan said, "Let's go."

Amherst nodded and then led him to her SUV. Bolan took shotgun. Amherst had just cleared the parking lot on the north side of the mall when they heard the first reports from units arriving at the scene of the Executioner's conflagration with members of the Thirteenth Street Gang. One of officers called in a make on the license plate of Bolan's rental less than a minute later.

Amherst cleared her throat as she rolled under the interchange and merged onto Slauson Avenue. "You mind telling me what the hell is going on?"

"I told you today why I'm here," Bolan said, deciding to play his cards close to vest. He liked her, but he didn't yet trust her.

"Yeah, I know. I got the party line about truth, justice and the American way. Listen, Cooper, if you want my cooperation you're going to need to start leveling with me. Do you really work for the DEA?"

Bolan smiled coolly and looked at her in the illumination from the dash lights. "Even if we were to say hypothetically that I don't, you know I couldn't tell you the truth."

"You could if you trusted me."

"I never said I didn't," Bolan said.

"You never said you did, either," she fired back.

The Executioner sighed. Okay, so he couldn't easily fool her. Amherst had been around awhile and he didn't have time for games. His instincts told him she wouldn't let up. She wouldn't interfere but she had enough intelligence and spunk to try digging into this thing without his confidence, and that wasn't something he could afford this early in his mission.

"Okay, here it is," Bolan said. "I work for people you don't know anything about, and trust me when I say it's better we keep it like that. As to why I'm here, it's simple. The kind of drugs you're talking about means major players are involved. I know one of the deceased on that boat was Kara Lipinski, and I also know everyone thinks these drugs are about gang rivalries and control over distribution territories. Given the recent number of successes you've had with minimizing gang activities, the last thing your higher-ups want to do is draw attention. But after what I learned tonight, I think you're way off."

"About what?"

"This isn't about gangs or local politics. This goes deeper...way deeper."

"Deeper how?"

"I don't know yet. What I do know is the gangs of Los Angeles don't have anything to do with it."

"And how do you know that?"

"Simple," Bolan said with a shrug. "Neither of the two bigwigs knew anything about the drugs. They were genuinely surprised when I mentioned pure heroin and opium."

"What makes you think it wasn't all an act?"

"I've been in this business awhile, lady," Bolan replied. "And that's not ego talking, it's fact. I've learned to read people pretty well, and I have an instinct for liars."

"So it was you who hit Antoine Pratt's place."

Bolan nodded and pressed his lips together in a grim mask. "I'm not trying to turn this town on its ear."

"Could have fooled me," Amherst said. She did nothing to hide the sarcasm in her voice. More gently, she added, "Although, that part of Ladera Heights you hit isn't within my jurisdiction, so it's no skin off my nose."

"How did you find out about Pratt?" Bolan asked.

She laughed. "I have ears all over L.A., Cooper. One of Pratt's men described a guy dressed, oh...a hell of a lot like you are right now. What I don't get anymore is exactly what you *are* doing here. You told me this afternoon Washington sent you here to run down the source of all this opium and heroin. You say you don't want me to tell my superiors you're here, but then you start firing up major gang leaders with explosives and automatic weapons, no pun intended. Just what's your angle?"

"You think I owe you an answer."

"I think I'm entitled."

"Not really, but your question's fair enough. I've been trying to decide if you're trustworthy."

"You haven't left me a whole lot of choices, either," she challenged.

"You want the truth, fine. I'm here to find out where these drugs are coming from. My guess is somewhere in Micronesia."

"Are you sure?"

"I will be as soon as I check out one more angle. The only question that remains after that is why the sudden rush."

"That's a good question," Amherst interjected. "Someone opened the flood gates and their timing's impeccable. It's not like I don't have enough problems on my hands. I'm short staffed right now due to budget cuts, and I have backlogged cases stacked as tall as Magic Johnson. To add to my worries, I have one mysterious DEA agent running around playing soldier."

"That's where you're wrong," Bolan countered. "I'm not playing."

"Neither am I," she said. "I won't keep pulling your bacon out of the fire, Cooper. DEA agent or not, fellow cop or not, this is your only freebie. Please don't ask me to continue keeping my mouth shut while you go around shooting up half the city. My loyalties to duty only extend so far, and I can't protect you forever even if what you're doing is right."

A tough mask fell across the Executioner's face. "I don't remember asking for protection. And I don't need your permission. You seem like a good cop, Amherst, but understand I have a job to do and that takes precedence."

"Look, I don't—"

"Someone's following us," Bolan cut in.

"What?" The Executioner saw her eyes go to first her rear-view mirror and then her side mirror, but she didn't move her head. "How do you know?"

"Part of that instinct I mentioned earlier."

"Who do you think it is?"

"I can't be positive but I think I have a pretty good idea," Bolan replied.

"What do you want to do?"

"Turn right at the next intersection," Bolan replied. "We need some running room."

"DAMN IT, BART!" Howard Starkey exclaimed. "They told us to lay off this guy. We should be back at the apartment watching TV or something."

Bart Wikert dragged a greasy palm across his face and cursed the heat. The air conditioner in their loaner unit had broken two days earlier, and their assignment hadn't permitted them time to wait at the Bureau's downtown offices while the motor-pool guys fixed it. Now he had to sit in this infernal metal sauna while listening to his partner bitch incessantly.

"Christ! This is great weather...if you're a fern."

Starkey chuckled at that and shook his head. "You're not very resilient to the heat, pal."

Wikert stared incredulously at his partner behind the wheel. "I'm from Vermont, moron! What's the big surprise?"

Starkey didn't reply, instead focusing on the road ahead, and Wikert decided to let it rest. The encounter with their alleged DEA cohort earlier in the day hadn't exactly left him in the spirit of cooperation. The ass-chewing he took from Wonderland earlier that day had put him in this foul mood. Who was Cooper that they should just stay out of his way? The events of the day, coupled with this heat, made him feel downright irritable enough to shoot the first stranger to piss him off. Wikert reconsidered the point and shook it off, almost laughing aloud at his ruminations.

"You know, buddy, this whole thing's ridiculous," Starkey said, intruding on his thoughts.

"Yeah," Wikert mumbled. "But I'm not going to accept we should just sit back and twiddle our thumbs. I don't give a damn what the DDO says."

The deputy director of operations for Homeland Security had instructed them to back off in no uncertain terms. "Don't rock the boat," he'd said, and that had been that. And all because somebody in the Oval Office had apparently called him within an hour of their meeting Matt Cooper and threatened to stick a hot poker into a private and uncomfortable place if they got another phone call. Well, Bart Wikert had nearly fifteen years with the FBI and he knew when something stank. This thing had one big odor.

"Listen, Bart, all we've done for the past six hours is watch Cooper run around this city and break practically every law known to man. Well, I for one am not going to just sit on my ass and do nothing. If the guy actually does hold legitimate employment with one of our agencies, then he's not following protocols. And if he works for the CIA, then he's operating illegally because we know they can't do shit within U.S. borders. So let's actually do something useful for once, get off our collective asses and get into the war."

"I didn't know we were fighting a war," Starkey replied quietly. There were moments that soft-spoken mannerism seemed so out of place on a guy of Starkey's size. In fact, it seemed almost feminine against that six-foot-four, 250-pound frame squeezed behind the wheel.

"Keep your eyes on them—they're turning onto that side street," Wikert replied. Then he continued, "It's a war as far as I'm concerned. This Cooper is breaking all the rules. So he has some clout with someone in D.C., so what! He obviously thinks he's a law unto himself and can break all the rules. Well, pride goes before the fall and I'm going to make sure we're there when he trips up."

As soon as they rounded the corner, Starkey had to stand on the brakes to avoid rear-ending the SUV they'd been tailing. The sudden stop nearly sent Wikert through the front windshield, since he would only wear a seat belt during high-speed pursuits. Wikert threw his right hand forward and caught his body with the dash, then let out a yelp of pain when he sprained his wrist.

Cooper emerged from the shadows of a commercial building with a pistol in his fist. He lowered the weapon as soon as it became apparent he recognized the pair. Wikert quickly recovered and rolled down his window when Cooper rapped his knuckles against it and gestured in a downward motion.

"What are you doing?" Cooper asked.

"What does it look like, asshole?" Wikert said. "We're tailing you."

"I thought we already settled this."

"Maybe *you* settled it. It's not settled for me yet. Not by a long shot."

"You're biting off way more than you can chew, pal," Cooper said. "If you're looking to borrow trouble, you've come to the right place. I know you have orders to keep out of my way, and I'd advise you to follow them."

"I don't take orders from you."

"I won't repeat this," Cooper said. "Back off."

With that, he turned and got into the SUV, and the vehicle drove away.

"Should I follow them?" Starkey asked.

Wikert said something under his breath but shook his head. There were other ways.

"What was that all about?" Amherst asked as she drove away.

"Some old friends," Bolan replied. He saw her check her mirrors again. "Don't worry. They won't follow us."

Amherst nodded. "So what's next?"

"Like I said before, I have one more thing to check out."

"I think I hear a *but* coming," she interjected.

"You do," the Executioner replied. "I need you to get me on that boat."

She let out a whistle. "You don't ask much, do you? Well, just so you know, I don't think I can get you onto that boat. It hasn't been fully processed by our crime-scene people, and as such it's considered to be in evidentiary lockup. I could only gain access now with a court order."

"Look, you've probably figured out by now I could make a phone call and get verbal authorization to get on that boat within ten minutes. But that would mean involving your superiors, and if they're in on this I don't want them knowing someone other than locals are involved. It would jeopardize my mission, and it would put you in a compromising position, too. So let's say we do this my way."

"Okay, but it isn't going to be easy. It's under constant guard. Even if my people agree to let me on board, they sure as hell aren't going to let you past, federal badge or not."

Mack Bolan grinned. "Who said anything about asking them?"

THE LUMINOUS GREEN NUMBERS on the digital wall clock read 3:23 a.m.

Although Barbara Price had perused Kurtzman's intelligence four times in preparation for briefing Hal Brognola, it still frustrated her. The mission controller shook her head as she scrolled through the data displayed on the twenty-three-inch LCD monitor in the Computer Room of the Annex at Stony Man Farm.

Price got frustrated when she couldn't seem to put her finger directly on something, even though she knew the answers were staring her in the face. Bolan, and the others in the field, Able Team and Phoenix Force, relied heavily upon her assessments. As mission controller, she gave the orders, after all. She had less of a hand where it concerned the Executioner—he called his own shots and they had an agreement on that particular subject—but he relied on Stony Man for his support. They couldn't mandate what missions Bolan could take or not take. The choices were utterly his. Yet he never hesitated to lend a hand when called upon, and so at the very least they owed him good, solid intelligence when he asked for it.

"How's it going?" a deep voice asked behind her.

Price jumped, then whirled in her chair. She felt her face flush. "What the hell is wrong with you? You scared the bejeebers out of me!"

Aaron Kurtzman drew back his head and raised his arms. Her uncharacteristic reaction didn't dawn on her immediately, but when it did she reeled back her temper and offered him an apologetic smile. She hadn't meant to bark at him like that. Kurtzman had turned out to be her closest friend and confidant, which wasn't surprising, since they spent many hours together at the Farm.

Kurtzman noticed her sheepish grin and accepted it as her way of apologizing. "My, my… Someone's jumpy."

"Not jumpy," she replied, shaking her head. She looked

back at the screen and sighed. "Just frustrated that I can't figure this all out."

"Well, I just came in to let you know Hal's back from Wonderland, and he's chomping at the bit."

"Probably more like chomping at his unlit cigar," Price said as she rose and scooped the computer printouts from the desk.

Kurtzman chuckled, then moved his wheelchair aside so Price could walk past. The click-clack of her heels reverberated off the walls of the hallway that eventually led to the underground tunnel connecting the Annex and the farmhouse. An electric car facilitated a faster transit time, but Price elected to walk the distance to clear her head, as well as to visit with Kurtzman.

"Any word from Striker?" she asked.

"Not since I talked to him earlier tonight."

"Actually, that was last night," Price reminded him with a wry grin.

"Touché." Kurtzman cleared his throat. "I take it the data I sent you wasn't that helpful."

"It's not the data, Bear," she replied. "It's my interpretation skills that seem to be off on this one. I can't make heads or tails of this thing."

"Well, maybe once you get it all out we can come up with something solid enough for Mack to work with."

Her voice seemed weaker as she replied. "Maybe."

They made the remainder of the trip in silence and within five minutes they were seated with Brognola in the War Room. The atmosphere actually made Price feel a little better, but it also caused her to realize how exhausted she really was. She hadn't slept in more than twenty-four hours.

The Stony Man chief smiled at her, but she could see something deeper beneath the surface. "What is it?"

"Nothing," Brognola said. "At least nothing I want to get into right now. What have you got?"

"I wish I could say lots, but unfortunately I don't know

how much more I can tell you than you probably already know from reading Aaron's intelligence."

"Just lay it out for me and let's see where it takes us," Brognola said.

"Sure. Well, to start with it would seem Striker was right about the Golden Triangle as being our most likely source for this opium and heroin. Its opium production exceeds four thousand metric tons annually, and Myanmar remains the largest contributor to that overall. In fact, Myanmar could probably satisfy the majority of world demand for heroin, which equates to about two hundred metric tons uncut."

Kurtzman whistled his surprise. "That's some serious dope." When Brognola and Price cast askance glances at him, he added, "No pun intended."

Price continued, "Opium production was pretty much a closed market based on geography up until about a decade ago."

"What changed?" Brognola asked.

"Mostly?" She shrugged. "Profit motive, I'd say. The various producers who had control of their regional territories decided they could all make more money if they pooled their resources in shipment and distribution. Since most of the north Asian and Middle East countries took second place when it came to places like Myanmar, they opted to defer to the Triangle for help and let them call the shots. Most of the product is now shipped into Taiwan and Vietnam, or smuggled south to Indochina, where it's processed, packaged and exported. Mostly to the West."

"Not that Southeast Asia doesn't have its share of heroin addicts," Kurtzman interjected.

"Of course," Brognola said. "But the difference is many of the users there who get hooked are the same ones actually helping pick the crop. It's how they make their living."

"And others manage to make their living by getting our kids and politicians and educators hooked on the stuff," Price said. "Like Hal said, it's mostly an economic way of life for those people. Third World countries regionally cultivate poppy with scant interference from legal or political entities, and in some cases no interference. Central and South American countries, and places like Lebanon, are no longer the up-and-comers of poppy production like most people believe. Vietnam, for example, cultivates more than three thousand hectares of opium poppy plants regularly. Only because they don't have the distribution system to support it do they have to funnel the majority of the product up through Taiwan and out of China."

"Okay, so I'd hazard a guess and say it's safe to assume Striker's on the money about the source of these drugs," Brognola said.

"I would agree with him one hundred percent," Price replied with a nod.

"Any ideas on who's behind it?"

"That's been sort of the gotcha," Price said. "There are any numbers of known overlords running the drug trade in the Golden Triangle. They're all big names and, as of late, all seem to remain untouched by any form of recognized law enforcement over there."

"Well, we've pretty much come to the consensus that the drugs are sourced in Myanmar. It shouldn't be too difficult to find out who's running things there and give that intelligence to Striker so he can act on it."

"That's the trouble," Price said. "We don't know whose operation it is anymore. Sung Suun was the man in charge up until about a year ago when he was killed during a police raid of his business holdings in downtown Pyinmana. Many of his competitors guess Suun's own underlings actually murdered him, at his request, because he didn't want to allow the authorities to capture him."

"Nice," Kurtzman said. "How did they cook up that theory?"

"I remember that," Brognola answered. "Our own intelligence people figured it was probably a publicity stunt more than anything else. They figured his little drug empire would hold together better if he went down as a martyr."

"And unfortunately," Price added, "nobody was left to contradict the stories of his 'heroic sacrifice,' since the punishment for drug trafficking over there is death. As soon as a trafficker's convicted, they take him out and put a bullet in the back of his head."

"Sounds like we could learn a lesson or two from Myanmar's government," Kurtzman replied.

"Hardly," Brognola replied with a snort. "Most of the public officials over there are just as corrupt as the dealers and drug lords."

Price nodded. "It's true. Whether anybody wants to admit it or not, drugs are a huge source of revenue for these people. They'll never get fair prices from the majority of the countries to which they export legitimate goods and services, and most American companies who farm out cheap labor to that side of the world do so because the standards for work conditions and facilities aren't nearly as stringent as they are here."

"That almost sounds liberal, Barb," Kurtzman said. "I'm surprised. I always took you for a conservative."

"I'm for the truth, which is what that is…right, wrong or indifferent."

"Okay, so Suun's dead," Brognola said with irritation evident in his voice. "What's our alternative?"

"That's where I'm totally stumped," Price said. "Under normal circumstances we would have discovered who Suun's replacement was and had our contacts keep tabs on him. But with the civil unrest that's taken place over there the past couple of years, we've had to cope with distractions on a wider scale. That's overshadowed our operations and made it much more difficult to keep our finger on the pulse of what's actually happening in Myanmar."

"Alternatives?" Brognola asked.

Price cleared her throat. "Well, I wasn't even sure I wanted to bring this up, but I figure it can't hurt to put anything and everything on the table at this point. One explanation might be that Myanmar is no longer the central point of production and distribution."

"Explain," Brognola replied quietly, furrowing his eyebrows.

Price reached to the printouts she'd brought and went right to a document halfway through the stack. "According to DEA statistics for just last year, America has a heroin-user population of more than two million people. That kind of demand has caused a sharp increase in opium imports. The primary crackdown area as far as the DEA is concerned has always been South American countries. Thus, most of our budget goes to operations there. That leaves the Southeast Asian heroin market wide-open. Most of drugs from the Golden Triangle come in through either maritime smuggling, mules over commercial flights or mail. The volume is simply too much for U.S. Customs agents to handle alone, and they aren't getting much support from other agencies."

Kurtzman shook his head. "Seems these days everyone's way more worried about bombs and anthrax coming through the mail than dope."

"Agreed," Brognola replied. "So where do you think we should focus our efforts, Barb?"

"Well, a good number of those export maritime operations come out of places like Borneo, Sumatra and so forth. That accounts for almost fifteen percent of our total oil and gas, electrical appliances, textiles and rubber imports. Hardly anything comes from Myanmar. For lack of any other evidence, I think we should be looking at Indonesia, specifically Jakarta."

"All right, start seeing what you can do about getting Striker a contact there." He turned to Kurtzman. "Bear, touch base with Cowboy and see if he has any friends left who might be able to help us out. I'd prefer not to go through official channels if we don't have to."

"I'm on it," Kurtzman said, and immediately wheeled himself out of the room.

Price and Brognola sat in silence a minute before Price said, "You want to let me in?"

"On what?" Brognola replied. He reached into the breast pocket of his jacket, withdrew a cigar and stuck it between his teeth.

"Don't be coy," Price replied. "What's going on, Hal?"

"Nothing, just a usual earful from the President." Brognola shrugged. "I guess he wasn't entirely happy about all the noise Striker's making. Apparently, he stepped on pretty big toes when he ran into that pair from Homeland Security."

"Striker can handle himself," Price reminded the Stony Man chief. "I don't think he considers them much of a threat."

"No, but the President's a bit close to this one because Simon Lipinski's daughter was killed. He wants results and he wants them quick, and he *especially* doesn't want to have a discussion about it. The last thing I need is for him to rag on me about Striker's thunderous, albeit effective, methods."

"I wouldn't worry about it, Hal," Price said as she rose from her chair. "Striker's there to get the job done and he'll come away with results. Whether the President likes it or not is irrelevant. We go through this almost every time. I've never seen you quite this affected by it. Did something else happen?"

"There are... Damn."

Price watched as something fell in Brognola's countenance. His face went pale, the expression morose, and light playing on those gaunt features and ghostly complexion aged him a good twenty years in the blink of an eye. Price had never seen him look more drawn and defeated than just in that moment, and it caused her heart to feel as if it might leap right up to her throat and lodge there.

Price swallowed hard. "My God, Hal. What is it?"

"The President received several official recommendations from members within his staff that he cease all sensitive operations outside of those conducted by sanctioned federal agencies."

"The President would never do that. I'm sure you can see that. I couldn't count on my fingers and toes the people who know about the Farm. Even the blacksuits aren't entirely aware of what goes on here. And how would these individuals even know about Stony Man anyway?"

"I don't think they do know," Brognola said. "Call it an educated guess, a fishing expedition. Maybe it's just a reactionary move, a political reach for lack of any other real control on the Oval Office. My guess is they're little more than lackeys riding on the coattails of some oversight committee member, and they're jockeying for position by calling out any discrepancy they can find."

Price shrugged and took her seat. "It all sounds like the standard cutthroat politics of Washington, D.C. I don't know why you're getting so worked up about it."

"Mainly because the Man said he's officially giving the proposal serious consideration."

Price caught her breath. *"What?"*

"It's true," Brognola said. "I had it checked out with my best sources."

"You have ears inside the White House?"

"Unfortunately, espionage is a necessary evil in this business." He lowered his voice, and added, "You of all people can probably understand that. We live in a time where you *have* to know where you might have enemies. While our operations remain mostly clandestine, there are occasions where Stony Man's security has been compromised. In those cases the lives of our people can become forfeit, and I won't allow that to happen. We've had our operations compromised before and it resulted in terrible, *ter-*

rible losses. I won't let it happen again if it's at all in my power."

"But why?" Price asked. For the first time she could remember in a very long time, she felt helpless. "We haven't given him any reason to disband Stony Man."

"He's the President. He doesn't need one."

Price swallowed hard. "This doesn't make any sense, Hal."

"None of it makes sense," Brognola replied. "For now, I want you to keep this quiet. Nobody's to know we had this conversation, including Striker. At least not until I've had some time to think about it. Is that clear?"

"It's clear." Price stood once more. "I'd better get to work. We need to put together some additional intelligence. We should be hearing from Striker soon."

She started to turn, then thought better of it, stopped and put her hand gently on Brognola's forearm. "This will all turn out okay, Hal. Trust me."

"This isn't going to work," Rhonda Amherst told the Executioner.

"Yes, it is."

Bolan sat on the edge of a dock approximately a hundred yards from the berth of Raul Montavo's yacht. Through binoculars, he'd observed a four-man detail of LASD deputies guarding the yacht. Two were stationed where the dock met the boardwalk, and the other pair roved the ten-foot chain-link fence that ran along the yacht-club perimeter. After timing their patrol, Bolan targeted a dark corner of the chain-link fence. Unless one of the roving officers got really close, he wouldn't notice the snipped wire at a corner post that was almost completely obscured by darkness.

"They're going to hear you," Amherst whispered with obvious tension.

"Only if you keep talking. Quiet."

Before proceeding to the marina, Bolan had Amherst return him to the airport to collect fresh munitions from his arsenal. He traded the FNC for the .44 Magnum Desert Eagle, and traded up the used Beretta with its spare. He also grabbed the wet suit from the all-purpose clothing packs stored aboard Stony Man's jet, then Amherst drove them to the yacht club.

"After seeing everything you've brought, my little Glock makes me feel almost naked," Amherst had remarked.

"I always hope they won't be needed," Bolan replied. "But mostly they are."

This way onto the boat hadn't been his first choice, but the Executioner didn't want to draw any more attention. He'd made enough noise kicking down doors in gang territory, and an unscheduled encounter with the LASD's men now wouldn't help his cause much. Mostly he had to depend on Amherst to play the part he'd instructed her to play. If it all went as planned, Bolan would be on and off the yacht within the span of a few minutes.

"I'm ready," he said as he zipped up the wet suit. "Start for the boat now. I'll meet you on the other side."

Amherst spared him another expression of doubt mixed with fear before she turned and headed down the boardwalk.

Bolan eased his body over the side and into the dark water. The calm ocean lapped gently against the dock support pillars. Bolan waited a minute beneath the dock to let his body adjust to the chilly ocean water. The cold felt good after the sweltering heat of the day and evening.

Bolan proceeded toward the dock after adjusting to the temperature change. He slithered through the ocean water, silent as an electric eel but many times more deadly. Bolan could detect voices by the time he reached Montavo's yacht. One he knew distinctly as Amherst's, and the other he assumed to be one of her men. Despite the fact the yacht remained in evidentiary holding, one of the philosophies behind that blue line continued to be "keep your mouth shut." The officers would not question their CO.

Bolan tried to get to a point where he could actually see Amherst, but his position just wouldn't allow it. After a minute or so he didn't hear anything else so he figured she'd passed muster. He quickly located the anchor chain, then as slowly and quietly as possible he pulled his body out of the water. Bolan dragged his way up the chain, arm muscles straining as he proceeded one agonizing foot after another until he reached the top. With a final effort, the warrior swung one leg over the top railing, then the other, and within seconds he was on the deck of the yacht.

The wind chilled the skin of Bolan's hands. He pressed his heels against the deck to drain the water from the neoprene soles of his waterproof boots. Bolan's gaze roved in both directions of the starboard deck, the side hidden from the pair of observers on the dock. Bolan rose and moved along the deck toward the stern. He came upon a set of short steps that descended into the lower cabin.

Bolan went down the steps and pressed his hand to the door. Something didn't feel right to him, but he couldn't figure out why. His sixth sense had put him on high alert, and the hairs stood up on the back of his neck. Theoretically, nobody should have been on Montavo's yacht, and yet the Executioner couldn't shake the feeling of someone else's presence. He also wondered what happened to Amherst; she should have joined him by now. Bolan checked the luminous hands of his watch and realized more than five minutes had elapsed.

He couldn't wait any longer.

Bolan reached for the handle and started to open the door just milliseconds before he sensed a malevolent presence loom behind him. Something rough suddenly encircled his neck and constricted his windpipe. The move would have completely cut his oxygen supply, but Bolan got his left palm against his neck before that happened. He reached to the combat knife sheathed upside down in leather on the harness of his LBE strap. He slapped the quick release and the knife blade dropped into his grip. Bolan twisted to his right as he pushed the garrote up and away, simultaneously driving the blade of the knife up and back. A muffled shout rewarded Bolan's efforts, and the tightening against his throat faded.

The soldier whirled to face his opponent, a wisp of a man with close-cropped hair, slanted eyes and a wide face. Bolan hammered a karate punch into the man's nose, then followed with a kick to the groin. The force of the kick lifted the smaller man off his feet and slammed him against the steps. The guy's head rapped against the fiberglass steps with a sharp crack.

Bolan sensed movement above and looked up to see a second man, this one about the same size, with one arm wrapped around Amherst's waist and an opposing hand clamped over her mouth. Bolan bounded to the deck in two steps and buried the knife to the hilt in the man's shoulder. The guy opened his mouth to scream, but the Executioner stopped it short with a rock-hard punch to the mouth. The blow dislodged teeth and sent them straight to the back of the guy's throat. He lost his grip on Amherst so she could finish the job. She drove an elbow into his gut, doubling him over and knocking the wind from him. A karate chop to the back of the neck nixed any further discourse.

Bolan lifted his eyebrows. "Something from your academy days?"

"Black belt in tae kwon do," she said with a shake of her head. "Sorry about that. They came out of nowhere before I could warn you."

"Forget it." He looked over his shoulder toward the dock. "Looks like the guard detail didn't hear us."

"Thank goodness for small favors," she quipped.

Bolan turned to the work at hand. He checked both men for identification but didn't find any—no surprise there. Both were carrying semiautomatic pistols with sound suppressors. Both had serial numbers, which surprised Bolan, so he memorized them for later reference and then tossed the pistols overboard. They made a faint splash. Bolan reached to a pocket inside his wet suit and withdrew two pairs of plastic riot cuffs, and from a second pocket a thin roll of duct tape. He bound and gagged the men quickly and then turned to see Amherst studying him with interest.

"Give me three minutes and then call for those guards," he told her.

"Three minutes? Is that going to be enough?"

"If I don't find what I'm looking for in two, I won't find it at all."

Bolan turned and descended the steps to the door once more, opened it and stepped inside. He closed it behind him, then clicked on a waterproof flashlight attached to the harness opposite his knife. Light filtered by a red lens spilled across the darkened interior of the main cabin. Bolan could make out the large stains of blood and outline markings of where the bodies had been found by crime-scene analysts. He dismissed the visions and concentrated on looking through drawers, under furniture and in every conceivable hiding place.

The hand of his watch swept just past the second minute when he found the wall safe behind a small painting. Bolan noted the three red numbers of an electronic display built into the door. He reached into his waterproof sack and withdrew a device created by Hermann "Gadgets" Schwarz, the resident electronics wizard of Able Team, Stony Man's urban commando unit. Bolan placed the device on the safe and typed an alphanumeric code into the keypad. Almost immediately the red digits began to cycle and had deciphered the code in eighteen seconds. The safe door detached with a soft click.

Bolan reached inside, grabbed the entire contents of the safe and dumped them into his waterproof satchel. He then secured the safe and replaced the picture. As he emerged from the cabin door and climbed the stairwell, Amherst began to shout for her men.

"Secure these guys and keep a lid on them," Bolan told her. "Don't let anybody question them. In fact, I'd get them alone and advise them to ask for a lawyer."

"Why the hell for?" she asked.

"To buy me some time," the Executioner replied.

And with that he left Raul Montavo's yacht at the same

point he'd come aboard. As he slipped into the chilly Pacific waters once more, the Executioner sensed his first real accomplishment since arriving in L.A. If Montavo had used the safe for what Bolan suspected he had, he would have the final proof he needed to track the drugs to their source. And then the warrior would hammer his enemy with an unforgettable vengeance.

The purveyors of death were about to feel the Bolan blitz.

"SO YOU THINK the source is Jakarta," Hal Brognola said.

"I know it," the Executioner replied.

The contents of the safe aboard Montavo's yacht had confirmed Bolan's suspicions regarding the origin of the opium, and it now left no doubt as to his next destination. Jakarta would not have been the soldier's first choice of target—the Asian drug cartel could be a formidable enemy. Under the circumstances, however, Bolan didn't see he had much choice. He'd promised to take this thing as far as he needed to bring closure to the death of Senator Lipinski's daughter, and to quell the massive tide of deadly product entering his country.

Bolan meant to keep that promise.

"Jakarta came up on our radar, as well."

"Really," Bolan said in his usual noncommittal fashion.

"Barb hit on what she thought was only a theory, but with what you've just added to the pot, I'd have to say that nails it as fact."

"I take it the Myanmar angle didn't pan out."

"It would have made sense if Sung Suun were still alive," Brognola replied. "Apparently he fell off the scope because he was killed by Myanmar authorities over a year ago, and executed any number of others who could have taken his place. That's reduced a bit of their maritime exports to the U.S., which left Barb to think Jakarta was where we should be looking."

"That cinches it," Bolan said. "You have any contacts in Jakarta?"

"I've instructed Barb and Aaron to touch base with Cowboy, see if he can pull any of his contacts from the DEA. Maybe he has some friends down there."

"An inside contact would narrow the playing field," Bolan agreed. "Jakarta's a big place. I'll be going in on a hunch as it is."

"Understood."

Bolan could hear something behind the sudden silence. "What's wrong, Hal?"

"Nothing."

"Bull," the Executioner shot back. "I've known you too long. You think I can't figure out when something's sour?"

"It's nothing to worry about, is what I meant."

Bolan didn't buy it. He'd known the Stony Man chief too long to think he would talk about anything going on back there. Brognola wouldn't want to bother Bolan with details or trouble him with issues that might not have any direct impact on the mission. Well, he'd find out sooner or later. A call to Price or Kurtzman could provide answers—he put it on his list of things to do as soon as time permitted.

Grimaldi's voice intruded from behind. "Sarge, we've got company."

"Have to go, Hal. Out here."

Bolan turned in time to see Grimaldi dive away from the entrance to the plane. The sounds of automatic-weapons fire and bullets pinging against the metallic skin of the jet told the rest of the story. Bolan rushed to the armory, slapped the M-4 carbine from the rack and loaded a magazine. He did the same with the M-16/M-203 combo and then rushed for the door. Bolan reached the door and looked out to find Grimaldi had taken cover behind the rear wheel of the plane. He tossed the M-4 to the pilot and then burst from the plane, hit the ground and rolled to his feet in a firing stance. The butt of the over-and-under combo held tight against his shoulder, cheek pressed against the stock, the warrior swept the open doors of the hangar for a target.

First Bolan spotted the lithe, uniformed form of Rhonda Amherst rushing his position, bullets biting at her heels. A van was parked behind her SUV, the side door open wide, the interior occupied by a half-dozen men in suits with an assortment of pistols and SMGs. Bolan had all he needed to act. He sighted on his targets and squeezed off a short burst.

Flame spit from the muzzle of the M-16 A-4 as the first pair of 5.56 mm rounds connected with a soldier on one knee who had taken careful aim on Amherst's back with a pistol. The rounds drilled through his chest and throat, then drove him against the opposite wall of the van with violent force.

Bolan's vicious response to the attack caused the assailants to reconsider their position. They were obviously no longer six well-armed men against a lone retreating female. Bolan took that moment to order Amherst to grab cover while Grimaldi let go with his first volley. The M-4 chattered as the Stony Man pilot directed a sustained burst of autofire at the van. As the assailants scrambled for the cover of the van seats, some of Grimaldi's shots found the skull of a second man and blew it wide-open. Flesh and brain matter geysered from the contact just a moment before the van door rolled forward and slammed closed. The last of Grimaldi's rounds skipped off the van door in a shower of sparks.

The engine roared, and Bolan took a moment to check the breech of the M-203. He could make out the brass-colored rim of the 40 mm HE M-383 grenade seated and awaiting deployment. Bolan closed the breech, flipped up the leaf sight, took aim and squeezed the trigger.

The weapon bucked with the kick of a 12-gauge shotgun, and the echo of a thunderclap filled Bolan's ears. Seconds passed and then the fleeing van exploded into a giant ball of red-orange flame. Secondary explosions followed as the van rolled to a halt and the heat ignited the gas tank.

Bolan rushed to Amherst as she regained her feet. "You okay?"

"Oh, sure," she said in a huff. She made a show of dusting her pants. "Never better."

Grimaldi showed up a few seconds later as Bolan continued studying her with a practiced eye. "Somebody like to tell me what the hell all that was about?"

"Later, Ace," Bolan said.

He gave Amherst his full attention. "I'm more interested in what you're doing here."

"What do you think?" she asked. "I've had no less than a dozen mucky-mucks in my office since before dawn, all asking a lot of uncomfortable questions."

"Our little friends from the yacht?" Bolan pressed.

"*Your* little friends, you mean," she said. "Of course, I managed to convince everyone I took them out single-handedly by catching them off guard, and since they're playing the 'we-no-speakie-English' game, it's in their best interests to keep quiet. Of course, all this work was when I actually thought you'd get with your friends back in Washington and get me some help. How naive of me."

"Sorry, but I was busy with something else," he replied.

"What?" she demanded with a mock expression. "A coffee break?"

"Look, lady, we—" Grimaldi began.

"Don't have time to get into that now," Bolan finished, eyeing his friend with a cautionary smile. "You haven't answered my question, Rhonda."

"Listen, I have a lot of superiors downtown, asking a lot of questions I don't have any answers for. What's more, I don't know what to do with these two thugs you somehow managed to take down single-handedly."

"All right," Bolan said, already concerned they would have enough to explain to airport authorities. "We've obviously stepped on some big toes. I found evidence in Montavo's boat that he was in Indonesia."

"How long ago?" Amherst interjected.

"Three weeks. We've agreed he brought the drugs back with him."

"He wasn't inspected by U.S. Customs?"

Bolan shook his head. "I don't think anybody even knew he'd left our waters. The yacht captain's log indicates he put out every day and was in by evening."

"And nobody even questioned it?" Amherst asked with total disbelief in her tone.

"Who, ma'am?" Grimaldi cut in. "Raul Montavo was a celebrity, well-known and highly respected in the Latin community, which, by the way, has no shortage of representation in California. Who's going to question the guy?"

"So where does that leave us?" Amherst asked.

"It leaves you here," Bolan said.

"Oh, no!" She shook her head. "You're not leaving me here to cope with this mess."

The Executioner frowned. "No arguments. You're a big girl. You'll handle it. It's my job to stop any more drugs from coming into the country."

"Sure," Amherst said with a scowl. "Ride off into the sunset and leave me holding the bag."

"What do you think's going on here?" Bolan fired back. "There's more to this than drugs, Rhonda. Somebody in Southeast Asia is trying to flood the market, and I have to know why before I can stop it."

"Fine," she said. "But what happened to interagency cooperation? What happened to you not wanting to tread on our turf?"

"I'm not treading, I'm leaving. The country."

"Say what?"

"I can't tell you exactly where I'm going, so don't ask," Bolan said. "Hold those two guys as long as you can. Trespassing isn't much of a charge, but maybe the fact it was a crime scene will gain you a friendly judge. And you can tell the politicians at city hall their secret's out. The DEA and FBI plan to flood L.A. in short order. Now, get out of here. I don't want your face around when airport security arrives."

Evening had transformed to early morning by the time Grimaldi taxied to a small hangar facility adjacent to the Soekarno-Hatta Airport in Jakarta. Unlike in other countries, Stony Man's influence didn't exactly reach to the heart of Indonesia or its neighbors, which dashed any hopes for the goodwill tour. Grimaldi and Bolan would both have to pass through customs.

They made sure by the time they reached the country that they looked the part. Bolan had thoroughly cleaned away the combat cosmetics and traded his blacksuit for a business suit of light, breathable cotton. Grimaldi greeted customs agents attired in a thrifty khaki-shorts-and-flowered-shirt ensemble. Sandals and a gaudy sports wristwatch completed his "I'm just here for fun in the sun" getup.

"Reason for your stay in Jakarta?" the slight agent in military-style uniform inquired.

"Business," Bolan replied.

"Women," Grimaldi added with a wicked grin. He jerked his head in the Executioner's direction and added, "And I'm his pilot."

The man studied the pair with an inscrutable gaze while Bolan looked at Grimaldi with mock indignation. Fortunately, the armory had a false wall concealing it, and most of the sensitive electronic equipment folded up against the sides of the fuselage, leaving only nondescript panels in their place. Not that it mattered, since the plane would remain at the airport.

And if the pair passed muster with customs there would be no reason to search the aircraft.

"Enjoy your stay in Jakarta, gentlemen," the agent finally said, stamping their forged passports before he returned them.

As soon as they collected their bags and headed for the main exit, the pilot remarked, "Something seemed off there."

"Yeah, I got the same feeling," Bolan said. "Keep your eyes open."

A car rental would have been convenient, but Bolan opted to go with public transportation instead. Not because it was cheap, but because it would be easier to notice someone out of place following them. The air-conditioned bus turned out to be empty save for a drunken old man, and within forty minutes they arrived in the downtown area. At first, the main road ran through predominantly residential sections but eventually they got to what Grimaldi referred to as *the civilized strip.*

"What's next?" he asked the Executioner.

"We find a hotel," Bolan said.

It took them only a few minutes, and Grimaldi did nothing to hide his pleasure at Bolan's selection of accommodations. Their hotel turned out to be one of the largest, both in size and capacity. It had a restaurant-lounge, suites and offered a significant array of services like grooming, tailoring and massages. It also advertised a facility providing guided tours, sporting activities and rentals.

Grimaldi dropped onto the deep couch, kicked his shoes off and propped his feet on an ottoman. He clasped his hands behind his head and leaned back against the arm of the couch with a sigh. "Now *this* is living it up. I'm beat."

"Get some rest," Bolan said as he dropped his suitcase inside one of the bedrooms and then headed for the door.

"What are you going to do?" Grimaldi inquired, watching Bolan with interest.

"I need some equipment. Kissinger gave me the names of a couple of guys who will probably have what I need."

"Want me to tag along?"

"No, better I do this alone," Bolan said. He stopped as he opened the door and added, "Like I said, get some rest. I'll be back in under two."

Grimaldi's eyebrows rose. "And if you're not?"

"Then I won't be back at all."

DESPITE THE COMPARATIVELY relaxed environment of Jakarta, criminal enterprises were intolerable to Indonesian officials. Laws had been less strict at one time, but the past decade or so had seen monumental shifts in the attitude of law enforcement and judicial authorities toward crime. Increased financial stability had contributed in large part to that shift, as well as world response to terrorism. Local and federal police agencies, not to mention the intelligence community, had reached a new sense of awareness. It wasn't as much that officials saw more as they had decided to *do* more about what they saw.

The Executioner couldn't say he minded, albeit unregistered firearms were now much harder to come by. Most weapons acquired through smugglers or the black market these days were cheap knockoffs or shoddy imitations. Gone were the days where he could know beyond any shadow of a doubt a Beretta was actually a Beretta, a Colt a Colt and so forth. The lines of honor weren't quite as narrow as they had once been, and even if he could acquire legitimate product it usually came at a hefty price. In fact, guns and other military surplus were often double the price per unit. All of these factors had made it necessary for Stony Man to keep a number of contacts under wraps in nearly every country, and Bolan would only deal with those he knew or who were referred by trusted colleagues.

Ihza Neechop happened to be one of those men. He'd served as a supplier to John "Cowboy" Kissinger during Kissinger's days in the DEA. Kissinger had also supplied Bolan with the contact who would help get him inside

Jakarta's drug empire, Sonny Tan, but that meeting wouldn' take place for several hours yet. The important thing now fo Bolan would be acquiring the tools of his trade.

The Executioner decided to grab another bus to tak him across town where Neechop conducted business. Nee chop's workshop—a small house in a quiet, run-dow neighborhood—sat on the western outskirts of Jakarta. Bola inspected the filth and poverty surrounding him on every sid as he ascended the rickety, dry-rot steps to Neechop's uncov ered stoop. He rapped at the door and waited nearly a minut before the door opened. A gray beard whipped in the breeze parted only by Neechop's toothless smile. His brown eye scrutinized the Executioner like the beady gaze of a mous deciding if it was safe to take the small cracker slathered wit peanut butter.

"You would have to be from Kissinger," he said in flaw less English.

"Yeah," Bolan replied. "And you would be Ihza?"

"Come in, come in," he said with the wave of his hand, nei ther confirming nor denying the Executioner's inquiry.

Bolan shrugged and stepped past the smaller man. H didn't suspect Neechop would give him any trouble. Th guy didn't make a living as an arms dealer by being a turn coat. He probably knew how to keep his mouth shut, and h had Kissinger's stamp of approval. That made him goo enough for Bolan. Kissinger wouldn't even have recom mended Neechop if there was any doubt in his mind abou the guy.

Neechop closed the door. "How is friend Kissinger?"

"He's good," Bolan said, surprised at Neechop's congeni ality. He wouldn't have ever suspected this guy of being major arms dealer. That fact actually made the Executione more comfortable with the transaction. "You were told of m requirements?"

It seemed that Neechop waved him away. "Yes, yes, o

course. I have everything you need. Your requests were simple. But there is, um…"

He didn't finish the sentence, just licked his palm, and he didn't need to; Bolan knew his direction. Neechop had concern for his payment. The Executioner couldn't really take offense. A guy like Neechop had to be careful in this business. Arms dealing didn't exactly qualify as the safest of professions. This guy had probably seen his share of punks, frauds and criminals all seeking an easy mark. In this case, it wouldn't have served either of them well to try cheating the other—both stood to benefit from offering a straight deal.

Bolan wouldn't have had it any other way. He reached into the deep pocket of his thin cotton shirt and withdrew a roll of bills. "Ten thousand U.S., small bills."

"That is perfect," Neechop replied with glee. He snatched the roll, pocketed it without counting, then motioned for Bolan to follow.

Neechop led the Executioner to the back of his hovel and opened a closet door. He looked back to see Bolan had followed, put his finger to his lips and then with a smile he pushed aside the mass of clothes dangling from the rack and merged with the darkness. Bolan stayed on his heels. He caught a glint of light and suddenly the light brightened and they descended a short flight of steps.

Within seconds he found himself in a cramped, dry basement where he had to duck to keep from whacking his head against floor joists. The place didn't exactly qualify as high tech, but it obviously had served its purpose well. The entire basement reeked of nitro solvent and gun oil. The walls were lined with SMGs and assault rifles of various makes, models and conditions. Neechop yanked back a greasy drop cloth from a table in the center of the tight quarters and slapped a switch near the wall that obliterated the overriding gloom with dramatic flare. An array of revolvers, semiautomatic pistols and a couple of machine pistols cast an oily gleam in way of reply.

"Kissinger said you prefer Beretta?" Neechop said with a teasing wink. He took a pistol from the table, locked back the slide and passed it to Bolan.

Bolan made a careful inspection of the 96 Brigadier Inox. The pistol differed from the 93-R in three main ways: no 3-shot burst, a satin-stainless finish and chambered for .40 S&W. Despite the potential limitations, it would still prove effective in the hands of a practiced marksman like the Executioner. Bolan nodded his approval at Neechop. The man immediately passed two loaded clips to him, a shoulder holster and an extra 50-round box of 165-grain semijacketed hollowpoint rounds.

"I'll need that SIG for my friend," Bolan said as he shrugged into the holster, loaded the pistol and seated it and the spare magazine in shoulder leather.

"Done." Neechop grabbed a nearby canvas bag and loaded it with the SIG-Sauer P-239. He included a spare magazine, Galco Jackass Rig and plenty of spare 9 mm parabellum rounds.

Bolan also selected an MP-5 SD-6—the silenced version of the MP-5 with 3-round-burst capabilities—and a SPAS-12 selective-fire combat shotgun. The shotgun wouldn't have normally been a choice for Bolan, but shotguns worked well in close-quarter urban environments and the Executioner wasn't yet sure what he'd encounter in Jakarta. Drug lords were very territorial, at best, and Bolan expected he wouldn't be welcomed with open arms.

Neechop bagged it all for Bolan in a nondescript canvas bag with a nonabrasive microfiber lining, then led him back to the main floor. They shook hands and Bolan departed. The soldier had managed to get half a block when he heard the squeal of tires on his flank. He turned in time to see a boxy vehicle round the corner of a side street and roar straight for him. It showed no signs of slowing, and when Bolan saw the front-seat passenger lean out and point a pistol at him, he knew they weren't there for a social call.

The Executioner dived to the broken sidewalk in time to avoid three rounds that buzzed over his head like angry hornets. He rolled once to clear the 96 Brigadier from its holster, and then got to one knee. He tracked the vehicle as it rolled past, leading only slightly, and squeezed off a double tap. Both rounds narrowly missed the shooter, but they were enough to keep his head down. The vehicle emitted a screech as the driver jammed on the brakes and made a sliding turn that brought the nose of the car in line with Bolan. The engine roared and the vehicle lurched forward. The occupants were obviously bent on ensuring Bolan didn't walk away from this encounter.

They were wrong.

Bolan raised his pistol and emptied the clip on the windshield. Had Bolan been firing 9 mm rounds, he might have only spiderwebbed the safety glass without actual penetration. The 96 Brigadier's .40 S&W rounds clearly had no such limitations as they punched straight through the glass. Three of the remaining eight rounds struck the driver in the neck and head. The vehicle, under control of the deceased, continued for Bolan's position. The warrior jumped to one side and let the vehicle continue onward until it struck a concrete stoop and stalled out.

Bolan slammed in the other clip as two native males with pistols burst from the backseat. A high-pitched whistle resounded through the air and steam spit from the radiator of the damaged engine. The front-seat passenger couldn't seem to get his door open, which bought Bolan some extra time. He sighted on the first target and squeezed the trigger. The bullet punched through the man's chest and dumped him on the dusty earth. The other gunman fired hurriedly at Bolan while scrambling to find some cover. The Executioner didn't concern himself with the shooter's pathetic aim, and instead focused on the moving target. He squeezed the trigger twice more and both rounds hit the gunman; one tore through his abdomen and the other shattered his right hip. The man's scream of surprise and pain rang shrill through the early-morning air and he hit the sidewalk face-first.

The other man had finally managed to escape the wounded vehicle and sprinted from it, trying to escape. Bolan, given his superior stride and strength, pursued the guy and easily caught him. The Executioner managed to catch the back of the man's knee and trip him. The man stumbled and fell, yelling as rough pavement left abrasions on his hands and knees.

Bolan stopped, bent and hauled the guy to his feet by his collar. The man tried to elbow Bolan, but the warrior deflected the blow with his fist. Bolan heard the faint but unmistakable click of a knife blade locked into an open position. He stepped back and waited for his opponent to make a move; the guy didn't disappoint. He lunged with almost clumsy disregard for his own defense, and Bolan took immediate advantage. He sidestepped the sharp blade and grabbed the man's right wrist with his left hand. Using his attacker's momentum, Bolan brought the man around in a circular motion, then stopped at the last minute and reversed direction with his entire body. The knife wielder's arm went one way, his body the other, and his elbow and wrist joints snapped with the torsion exerted on them. The man screamed and dropped the knife. He landed on his back, and Bolan finished it by dropping onto the man's sternum with his knee. The chest collapsed, ribs cracked and fractured bones punctured the lungs and heart.

The Executioner got to his feet, somewhat winded by the encounter. He'd only been in-country a couple of hours. He couldn't believe someone would know about his presence already. The drug network in Jakarta was good, but it wasn't that good. Still, this hadn't been some random attack by fanatics. These men had been sent with one purpose in mind: to kill him.

Bolan got out of the area quickly before the Jakarta police showed up. He didn't need to be in contact with them, especially not toting that kind of illegal firepower. He quickly returned to the dropped bag and headed for the hotel. He could only hope Cowboy's contact would be able to provide some answers.

"OUR MEN FAILED, sir," Jarot Pane said quietly.

"How?"

"We are not sure."

"How many did you send?"

"Four," Pane replied.

"And how many did you lose?"

Pane swallowed hard. "Four."

"Pathetic," came the reply. "Perhaps you have learned a lesson from this."

"What lesson would you have me learn?"

"It is foolish to underestimate your enemy."

"You're saying I should have sent more men?"

"I am saying you should have sent competent men." There was a pause. "Instead, you figured one man would be an easy target. Did I not caution about this man before I gave you the assignment?"

"Yes, sir."

"And did I not tell you he was from the American government? And that he had single-handedly created significant unrest among our operations in Los Angeles?"

"Yes, sir."

"Why, then, did you doubt me, Jarot? Have I given you some reason to doubt me?"

"No, guru, of course not!"

Jarot Pane stood before his teacher and master—the fearless leader who had brought all of them wealth and prosperity—with his head down. He could not look at his guru; in fact, he dared not look at him. He had not listened and thus he had failed, and so he deserved whatever punishment might befall him. Fortunately, his teacher had repeatedly demonstrated his capacity for mercy. Pane waited to see what would become of him.

The guru rose and put a hand on Pane's shoulder. "I know one of those men was your nephew. I understand the pain you feel. Your brother died years ago in service to this same cause, and you swore an oath to protect your nephew. That is punishment unbearable for most any man. I will not punish you further."

Jarot Pane tried not to show his relief, but he knew he couldn't fool his master. Intelligence was simply part of the guru's breeding. He could no more turn this off than he could murder one of his own. Pane had served under him for two years now, and he knew his master's limits. Maybe one day there would come a time where he could no longer tolerate Pane's failures, but today would not be that day.

"Now, we must teach this American that he cannot simply come here and operate with impunity. I cannot tolerate or permit his interference. We have made promises to certain people, very *powerful* people, and they will not allow us to simply ignore the problem."

"What do you wish me to do, guru?"

"Nothing. I'm going to deal with this man personally. I have already made all of the necessary arrangements. You will continue to oversee our operations here. The heroin must get to Los Angeles as scheduled. Our partners won't be able to proceed with their operations if we fail to hold up our end of the bargain. Not only would that ruin our financial prosperity, but it would utterly destroy my reputation as a businessman of his word. Do you understand me?"

"I understand."

"Excellent." Pane's teacher clapped his hands twice in rapid succession. "Now, get on with your work. And I no longer want you to worry about this Matt Cooper. Before I'm through with him, he will have learned the price of our blood."

So swore the Golden Dragon.

"You must be Cooper," Sonny Tan said as he entered the hotel room.

Bolan closed the door behind him and the pair shook hands. Tan didn't really stand out on first impression, which had probably been to his advantage. He stood at average height, maybe five-ten, and possessed a medium build. Dark eyes, shaped to betray just a hint of his Asian lineage, darted around the room. He wore a pair of cream-colored slacks, tan loafers and a yellow polo shirt. The Executioner introduced him to Jack Grimaldi by first name only, then the three of them sat at a square table near the sliding-glass doors of the patio over coffee and rolls.

"Give me the lowdown on the drug trade here in Jakarta."

Tan blew out a gust of air, sat back and ran his hands through his dark buzz cut. "Where the hell would you like me to start?"

"How about with who's in charge?"

"That depends on who you ask," Tan said. "If it's the local authorities, they'll tell you most of the major action is split among a bunch of different drug lords. And none of them is really higher than the other. It's how they justify not having been able to crack the Asian pipeline through the Triangle."

"You mean, by claiming it's more difficult to bring down a group of smaller fish than one big one," Bolan interjected.

"Exactly."

"What about you and your people?" Grimaldi asked. "What's your take on all of it?"

"We're pretty sure there's one man behind most if not all of the action in this part of the world. We've never been able to put a name or face on him, but he goes by the name Golden Dragon. Because he's remained anonymous for so long, the Indonesian cops have managed to convince their superiors he's nothing but an urban myth."

"But you beg to differ," Bolan said.

"You're damn right I do," Tan said with conviction. "Trying to prove the Golden Dragon exists to these people is like trying to prove racial equality to a racist. It all makes sense, and everyone knows the facts, but they'll stick to their guns because it's what they *want* to believe despite mounds of evidence to refute it."

"Ignorance is the first, greatest stepping stone to utopian bliss," Grimaldi replied.

"Who said that?" Tan asked.

The pilot grinned. "I did just now."

"Going forward," Bolan cut in, "what kind of evidence have you gathered the Golden Dragon exists?"

"Only talk on the streets," Tan said. "We tried several different times to notify Indonesian officials about potential manufacturing and storage sites all through this city. Every time we get a tip, we pass it on to them, and every time they make a raid they come up with zero."

"Sounds frustrating," Grimaldi remarked.

"Sounds like a mole," Bolan said.

"Where?" Tan asked. "Inside the DEA?"

"Not likely," Bolan said. "I'd guess your operations are too small and close-knit for someone to successfully get a mole inside. At least to keep them there for any length of time."

"You think the leak is inside Jakarta law enforcement."

"It's a good bet," Bolan said. "We got into the country with very little effort."

"Yeah," Grimaldi added helpfully. "Customs officials were almost, well...polite to us."

"I made contact with one of our other people," Bolan continued, "and ran into trouble as I was leaving his neighborhood. It was no accident. They didn't just happen on me."

"What did they want?" Tan asked.

"To terminate my stay."

"Well, nobody on my team even knows you're in-country yet. It couldn't have been one of our people."

"I'll get to the bottom of it eventually," Bolan replied. "Meanwhile, what else can you tell me about this Golden Dragon and his operations inside Jakarta?"

"Well, he's apparently well connected with every kind of person you can imagine. He knows lawyers, prominent businessmen, teachers and even politicians. He has a whole network of street workers in his pockets, everything from prostitutes he uses as his eyes and ears to the menial laborers in factories, restaurants and hotels."

"So a hotel employee might also have spotted us coming in," Grimaldi said, looking at the Executioner for an opinion.

"Maybe," Tan replied.

"Go on," the Executioner said.

"The Dragon doesn't appear much for vices, either, which has made it hard to garner a profile. It's been alleged he doesn't drink, smoke, do drugs or solicit female companionship. His standards are said to be very high when it comes to food and drink, and has very eclectic tastes in decorum. Word has it his hired help call him *guru,* which you may or may not know is Malay for *teacher.* Outside of the fact he's rated one of the most notorious criminals in Indonesian history, we don't know a damn thing about him."

"At least nothing of any use," Grimaldi added.

"Maybe not," Bolan countered.

"Uh-oh." Grimaldi produced a wan smile. "I've seen that look before, Sarge. You've got something."

"Maybe," Bolan said. He looked Tan in the eyes. "You said he's not known for being a ladies' man."

"Yeah?" Tan shrugged. "So what?"

"That means he might prefer men. Maybe even boys."

Tan said nothing for a long moment, his face pondering the consideration. He finally said, "We'd thought of that, but ultimately we dismissed it because of his background. He was supposedly raised in a very strict, traditional family and such behavior wouldn't have been tolerated."

"Maybe not," Bolan said. "But people change. And who could stop him? You just said he's infamous throughout the land."

"It's a possibility, I suppose," he said. "I won't dismiss it entirely. I'll see what I can find out about it for you."

Bolan nodded. "Fine. For now, though, I'd like to hear more about these areas of operation you pointed to. You said Indonesian authorities were never successful on any of these raids?"

"A couple of times they caught some users, but they were low-level street punks. Half didn't even know the names of their suppliers, and the other half wouldn't have said anything if they did. You've entered a secret society, fellas. I'd recommend you don't try to probe the area without being accompanied by me or one of my people. You wouldn't get far."

"How come they talk to you?" Bolan asked.

"Fair enough question," he said. "And simple. They trust me."

"Because?" Bolan pressed.

"Because they know I'm not looking to bust them."

"Or at least they know you have no authority to bust them," Grimaldi said.

Tan shrugged and splayed his hands. "I could turn them over to the locals. You know, you can do five years in jail for possession of just a half ounce of heroin in this city. Not to mention the beating they're going to throw you when nobody's looking. You ought to see the ratio of those arrested who come in having gotten the living shit kicked out of them because they allegedly resisted."

"I'm not surprised," Bolan replied.

"Out in the country lands, they couldn't care less about who's doped up. Here in Jakarta, though, they care very much. Streets filled with dope fiends tend to affect tourism and trade. Anyway, I don't rat out my contacts because eventually I'm going to get the truth out of one. If I betray those people, they'll never talk to me, and there goes my one chance to bring down the Dragon."

"Unfortunately, it doesn't sound like your current tactics have gotten you that far," Grimaldi remarked.

Tan expressed offense at Grimaldi's comment. "Don't criticize *me,* pal. I've been sweating it out down here in this shithole for one hell of a long time. I deserve some respect."

"Settle down," Bolan said. "He didn't mean any disrespect. All he's saying is the present methods aren't working. Understand I'm on a time budget, Tan. I think maybe I can help you out with this. You can have the credit if we catch him. My only concern is stopping the flow of drugs into Los Angeles's ports."

Bolan's words seemed to satisfy him. "Sorry. I'm a little edgy of late. It's getting tougher here, and my job's on the line because we're not meeting our bosses with tangible results. If I get yanked out of here for being nonproductive, my career's finished."

"Well, don't start packing yet," Grimaldi replied easily. "I think the sarge here has a plan."

"Cool." Tan looked at Bolan. "How can I help?"

"Tell me what you know about Raul Montavo's visit here a few weeks ago," Bolan said. "You knew he was dead?"

"I heard," Tan said with a nod. "Couldn't have happened to a nicer guy."

"Did you see him with a young girl? White?"

"Yeah, as a matter of fact. I figured it was just another one of his squeezes."

"She was a senator's daughter," Bolan replied.

"Simon Lipinski, of California," Grimaldi added.

"Shit," Tan said. "If that's true, then you're not going to believe what I'm about to tell you guys."

The Executioner's face went hard. "Try me."

SONNY TAN WAS RIGHT. The tale he told Bolan and Grimaldi sounded unbelievable. Yet it all made sense. Despite Raul Montavo's star status, the guy was a "big-time dope fiend." That fact wasn't public knowledge—it hadn't even gotten into the tabloids—and apparently only a few close friends even knew about his drug use. Over the years, Montavo had allegedly burned a number of his suppliers, either haggling over price or not paying them at all, due to his gambling problem.

"The young lady who accompanied him had that same problem," Tan said, "except she liked to gamble on men. You see, we noticed immediately she wasn't shy to spend other people's money, and Montavo apparently didn't seem to mind. She had her own clothes, her own chauffeur over here, even her own credit cards that he apparently signed for. They ate in the nicest restaurants, stayed in the best hotel and toured the finest art galleries and clubs in town."

"How does that happen?" Grimaldi asked. "How does a nice young girl end up with a dirt bag like that, and nobody even says 'boo' about it. Especially her influential father who, by the way, has ties that reach far and wide."

The Executioner knew the answer; he'd seen this type of thing time and again. Being eighteen years old meant Kara Lipinski had legal independence. She didn't answer to anyone, and she didn't have to do anything she didn't want to. The girl could vote, hold down a job, whatever. She couldn't legally drink in the U.S., but there would be no such restriction imposed over here, and considering Montavo's influence it didn't really matter anyway.

The most puzzling aspect of the whole thing centered on why a sweet girl like Kara—who had everything going for her and the intelligence to do anything she wanted—would ultimately "hook up" with a cad like Raul Montavo. While he remained the Latin sweetheart of Hollywood, Tan indicated Montavo had a reputation for spending days in a drug-induced stupor where he could not eat, drink or even perform sexually. This had apparently been a source of contention between Montavo and Lipinski, and resulted in more than one argument. Montavo had apparently never touched her, but sources had told Tan that they witnessed Lipinski's penchant for violence firsthand.

"Apparently she would throw furniture, slap him around, all kinds of shit," Tan said. "I also heard she could swear like a sailor."

Bolan wasn't sure how much he bought anything he'd been hearing until Tan began to tie it together for them. Drugs had been the primary reason for Montavo's visit to Jakarta. He'd apparently run low and decided to look for a fresh supplier. Since he'd burned most of his local contacts in L.A. and getting supplied from some other dealer in a nearby city spelled more risk than he cared to absorb, Montavo got it in his head to come to Jakarta to buy in bulk. He'd apparently offered to let Lipinski accompany him, and the two sailed out on his yacht three weeks earlier.

"I hadn't heard about his death until my friends back in D.C. called me saying an old comrade was trying to reach me. Once I heard John needed a favor, I dropped everything to get involved. I figured this would be news to you, too."

"So why do you think someone shot them up?"

Tan sighed. "Where do I start? For some time now we've suspected an increase in the Dragon's export operations. The guy has been manufacturing and cranking this stuff out for a while. But like I told you before, we still haven't been able to find anyone who can tell us exactly where his operations are or what kind of real volume we're dealing with. It's all been guesswork and conjecture based on limited and shaky intelligence. People are more afraid of the Golden Dragon than they are of the cops. And that's saying something in a place like Jakarta."

"What about externally?" the Executioner asked.

"What do you mean?"

"Is there product coming into Jakarta from other places? Maybe this Golden Dragon isn't doing any of the manufacturing. Maybe he's acting as a pipeline for everyone else."

"We considered that, but it doesn't seem likely. Any drugs that would come into this area would be competition. He'd lose money if he allowed others to use him as a pipeline. If he acts only as a distributor, there wouldn't be enough cash in it for the risk. He could probably get fifteen...maybe twenty percent at the outset."

"You're right," Grimaldi said. "That isn't much profit."

Tan nodded. "Yes. We think he'd stand to make a lot more through manufacturing. That way he could harvest the crop, process, package and ship the product at a nominal cost and still make much more profit in the end. There might once have been a time in this business where distribution stood to be profitable on its own, but these days it's much less likely when you consider the risks. Maybe you could make some cash with a cut of thirty-five or forty percent, but the majority of suppliers aren't going to give the shit away."

"None of this explains the connection between Montavo and Lipinski," Bolan said. "And why LASD discovered a boatload of bodies at Montavo's yacht club in Marina del Rey."

"Like I said, Montavo came to Jakarta specifically for the purpose of buying drugs. There was some sort of communications breakdown. We didn't know why he was here. Our contacts back in Hollywood told us he was out here on vacation, between films or something. By the time we found out why he was actually here, he'd already left."

"With the drugs," Grimaldi said. He looked at Bolan. "I think someone found out about it and tried to hijack him for them."

Bolan shook his head. "No dice, Ace. They left the drugs behind. Somebody was there strictly for the purpose of killing Montavo. Based on what we've heard, I think it's because he met the Dragon."

"Nobody's met the Golden Dragon," Tan muttered under his breath.

The Executioner got to his feet. "Somebody's met him, because people know he exists. He obviously has a stranglehold on this city, and whether he's making his own dope or getting it from the outside, I'm here to shut him down before anybody else dies."

Tan emitted a whistle. "That sounds like a tall order."

"It's not," Bolan said. "I need your help, though. I want a list of every area where you received a tip and the Indonesian authorities came up bust."

"What are you planning to do, Sarge?"

"I'll feed the info back to the Bear," Bolan said. "That ought to give me a good starting point. And then I'm going to follow up on a lead of my own."

IT TOOK KURTZMAN only two hours to come back with the information Bolan sought. Bolan had been to Jakarta a number of times through the years, and he had some familiarity with the area. He knew the only way to flush out the Golden Dragon would be to hit the guy hard. Based on Kurtzman's list, what information he'd gleaned from Tan and his familiarity with the Jakarta underworld, the warrior figured he had enough to go on.

Bolan's search started on the east side of the city, near the waterfront. His battle plan was to hit the distribution areas first; in effect, that would clog the pipeline. In turn, he would probably pick up enough intelligence along the way to lead him back along the distribution trail. Eventually, that would get him to the point where he could ascertain the source of the operations, which would lead him to the Golden Dragon.

Bolan understood the myth of the Dragon. He'd been a myth himself, once, during his operations against the Mafia. That seemed like a dozen lifetimes ago in his War Everlasting, and yet somehow there were moments that seemed like only days or weeks had passed. Occasionally he would think of those who had fallen. All of them had died fighting against terror and crime and repression; all of them had died living large. In a way, that made them myths, too.

The Golden Dragon stood as a different kind of myth, though. This man, whoever he was, stood for nothing but degradation and humiliation of society in promotion of his own desires. Self-aggrandizement had long served as the tripping stone of criminals, terrorists and dictators throughout world history. Bolan felt confident the Golden Dragon would prove no exception to that rule. The most important thing now would be to find his operations and shut them down as quickly as possible. As far as the Executioner was concerned, the Golden Dragon's reign was about to end.

The time had come for a Bolan blitz in Jakarta.

Rhonda Amherst tried to devise some reasonable explanation for the events of the past two days, and to explain her conduct in hiding the truth from her superiors. Unfortunately, she didn't have much to say on either topic. That quickly led to her suspension pending a review board, which the department legally had to provide her within seventy-two hours.

Amherst parked her SUV in front of her small home and went inside. She locked and bolted the door behind her, dropped her keys on the table, and then—stripping off her clothes as she went and leaving them where they fell—headed straight for a much needed shower. Ten minutes later she exited the bathroom, one towel draped around her body and the other wrapped swamilike on her head, and checked the answering machine.

Nothing.

Amherst tried not to let the disappointment ruin her day. Oh, hell, who was she kidding? The chief and county commissioners had already managed to do *that.* Cooper not having called bothered her most, although she didn't know why. She could only assume he was busy or just not where he could contact her. She didn't even want to think about the third alternatives. After the way she saw him handle her attackers at the airport, she knew he could take care of himself.

Amherst toweled dry her long dark hair, slid into a pair of loose-fitting denim shorts and a white silk tank top and then sat at a quaint vanity table and began to brush her hair. She'd bought the table from a secondhand store, despite the fact it wasn't her style, because it reminded her of her mother. She studied her features as she brushed and realized she looked gaunt—she attributed that to near exhaustion.

The phone jangled her from her daydreaming. She dropped the brush on the table and raced to the phone. She stopped and calmed herself, clenching her fists repeatedly and steadied her breathing. She picked up the receiver midway through the third ring.

"Hello?"

"Captain Amherst?" came a gruff, official-sounding voice.

"Speaking." Amherst's suspicions immediately rose.

"My name is Harold Brognola," he said. "You don't know me, but right about now my plane is headed into Los Angeles. I need to meet with you as soon as possible."

"Regarding?" she said.

"Matt Cooper."

"I apologize, Mr. Brognola, but I don't know anybody—"

"Yes, you do," he cut in. "I *know* you know who Cooper is. I also know the kind of trouble you got into on his account. I'm here to help you rectify that. But I need to meet with you."

"Look, I've already told you I don't know any Cooper," Amherst said. She remembered his telling her to distrust everyone. "And I haven't slept in over twenty-four hours, so if you don't mind—"

"Amherst, my flight will be touching down within the hour. I'll be at the exact same private hangar where Cooper was. You can either meet me there or not. I'm sure he probably made no mention of me, and told you not to trust anybody. But understand this—I need your help and so does he, and I'm giving you the opportunity to get involved. Cooper told me that's what he thought you wanted. Now, is it or isn't it?"

"Yes," she said quietly.

"So will you meet me?"

"Fine, but not there. I'm too popular these days."

"Okay, fair enough. You name the place."

HAL BROGNOLA HADN'T really expected Amherst to agree so readily to a meeting, so he'd gone into high alert. He hadn't operated in the field for some time, but in his mind he could still hold his own. A little slower and a bit older, but that didn't matter to the big fed because like it or not, his friend was out there putting it all on the line.

As he walked into the seaside restaurant that could have doubled as a frat house, Brognola could only take a small measure of solace in the .45-caliber Colt Combat Commander concealed in a hip holster beneath his suit jacket. One look at the denizens of the pub and Brognola felt a hundred years old. Even though he had Amherst's general description it still took him nearly five minutes and two walk-throughs before he located her. He figured from the corner table she occupied in a darkened corner that she had seen him on the first pass and decided to wait for him to find her.

Brognola put out his hand as he sat, but Amherst only looked at him through eyes as dark as her hair. The Stony Man chief shrugged it off. "Suit yourself. Thank you, though, for agreeing to meet with me."

"I haven't agreed to stay yet."

"You will when you hear what I have to say."

"I don't want to seem like a prude, but do you have some sort of official identification, Mr. Brognola?"

Brognola couldn't resist a smile as he withdrew, slowly and carefully, his credentials and badge with the Justice Department and dropped them on the greasy wooden table between them. "You are a tough one, just like Cooper said."

Amherst picked them up and studied them a minute. "Justice...impressive," she said as she returned them. She shook her head in disbelief. "'All the king's horses and all the king's men.' Washington never ceases to amaze me."

Brognola entertained just a moment the thought of telling her to lose the attitude under the auspice of pulling rank, but ultimately he opted against it. Amherst had been through enough. She was a good cop, according to Bolan, and he could hardly expect her cooperation if he berated her for getting a bad rap.

Amherst folded her arms on the table in front of her and leaned forward some so she didn't have to shout over the music. "So, I suppose right about now you think I should be yessir-ing you all over the place. Show the proper respect."

Brognola couldn't repress a smile this time. "I got used to no respect a long time ago, Amherst. But understand, I'm as committed as Cooper to this mission, and I've paid my dues. You can be sure of that."

"So you're not here to burn me after all."

"I'm not," he replied.

She leaned back, crossed her arms and studied him. The music had faded to a less raucous ballad. "All right, I'm being a bitch. Can you blame me?"

Brognola shook his head.

"What do you want, then? You said it was important. I'm tired and I don't have time for guessing games."

"I'll pass the first olive branch by telling you that for all intents and purposes I work for the Justice Department, yes. Off the record, I do a little more than that. I work for powerful people. People well above your pay grade."

"Is that meant to scare me, Brognola?"

"It's meant to wake you up," the Stony Man chief said. "We're not playing some game here, lady. The same people who have been putting drugs into this country over the past few weeks at an alarming rate are the same kind as the pair you have locked up. And they're the exact same kind who wouldn't hesitate putting a bullet right between those pretty brown eyes of yours. So listen up. I need your help and you're going to provide it, and provide it willingly, or I'll lock your ass up. You in or out?"

"I don't have to like it, I just have to do it. Is that the deal?"

"That's the deal."

Amherst appeared to chew on that awhile. Brognola hadn't planned to come in quite so hard, but he had less time than he had about seven minutes ago, and he couldn't take much more of it. Every minute he spent fencing with Amherst meant one less minute he had to provide Bolan the support he needed and prove to the Man that Stony Man's operations had to remain intact.

"How do I know you're not just another one of those vultures looking for your next scapegoat?"

"You don't," Brognola said flatly. He lifted his eyebrows. "But how much more trouble do you think you could get in than you are already? At this rate, I could only improve your situation. Wouldn't you say?"

"All right," she said without another thought. "I'm in."

"Good." Brognola removed two photographs from his pocket and handed them to Amherst. "You recognize either of those men?"

"Yeah," she said. "They're the goons I have on ice at county lockup. Cooper told me to find anything to keep them that way."

"He's right," Brognola said. "The bigger one there goes by Maki Santoso. He's a coward and thug from Indonesia, wanted by Jakarta police on at least a half-dozen charges of trafficking and murder. You know what drug-running buys you in many parts of the Golden Triangle, Amherst?"

The police officer shook her head slowly.

"A bullet in the brain. The second man is Shihab Hamzah, a known Muslim terrorist and member of the Jemaah Islamiyah. Ever heard of them?"

Amherst nodded. "Some. I hear the JI have been a pain in our collective asses."

"That's putting it mildly. It's no wonder a group like the JI is able to operate in Indonesia. The entire area has the largest concentration of Muslims anywhere in the world. The government is filled with corruption, and the maritime borders are run in as carefree a manner as Coney Island. And unfortunately, I'd have to say too much time has passed for the world to still be able to blame the Dutch for the fiasco there. So, now you have some idea of the kinds of people you're dealing with."

"So how do I fit into all of this?"

"Much as I hate to say it, we needed a fall guy. You were our most opportune choice under the circumstances."

"Why?"

"You already had suspicions about your superiors, and from everything I could find out you didn't exactly try to hide that fact. Particularly from them. It seemed logical they would target you when they found out you went back to Raul Montavo's yacht and were just lucky enough to happen onto Santoso and Hamzah. And by the way, nobody believes you."

"Yeah," she said, rolling her eyes. "I kind of got that impression."

"What I don't want you to do is worry," Brognola told her. "This whole thing was by design. It had to be that way, which is why Cooper gave you the instructions he did."

Amherst cleared her throat. "I don't suppose you can tell me who you really work for."

"No, I can't. Let's just say I'm one of the good guys, for now, and we'll play the rest by ear."

"So why all the espionage? And when do I get my secret decoder ring?"

"Funny," Brognola deadpanned. "We needed them to dismiss you temporarily so you could help us determine the link to the Golden Triangle drug ring on this end."

"The 'link'? What the hell are you talking about?"

"Let me back up," Brognola said. "Fill you in on maybe some things you don't know. It's no accident you and Cooper stumbled on your two friends at that boat. You see, we were convinced pretty early on there was more to this than just a simple drug-smuggling operation. The sheer volume and purity of the stuff tells us that."

"It sounds like you're trying to tell me things are about to get more interesting."

"Right. If Santoso and Hamzah are anything, they're an indication the drugs are only a secondary concern. It would seem someone's trying to flood the U.S. heroin and opium market, and in a product volume greater than we've ever seen. At this point, my boss wants it taken care of."

"And I don't suppose you could tell me who that is, either?"

"When he says jump, everyone asks, 'How high?' That a good enough answer?"

"It'll do," she said. "So why me?"

"Why you what?"

"Why did you choose me to be your little sacrificial lamb? Just so you could get me by the short hairs and tell me what to do?"

"Nothing of the sort," Brognola said. "In fact, the opposite. You can walk away any time you want, Captain. But my gut and the file on you both say you won't. And who better to help us out with Los Angeles County than an experienced LASD officer? We were very careful when we selected you."

"Okay, so you know some things about me. What do you need me to do?"

"Tell me where to look, how to get inside, anything at all that will help us nail it down so we can determine where the real threat has taken up residence."

"You have a team in mind?"

"Yeah," Brognola replied quickly. "We're it."

Amherst's eyes went wide, betraying the fact she could hardly believe what she had just heard. "Are you nuts? I'm a cop on suspension and you're… Well—"

"What? Too old?" Brognola had to laugh at that one.

"Young lady, I was busting the heads of street punks before you were born. I've been a cop for more years than I want to count. And I may have been born in the dark, but it wasn't last night. A lot of cops work for me. I know what it means to be a cop, and to supervise cops. So cut me some slack and give me the benefit of the doubt, huh?"

"Sorry," she said. "The odds just seem a little overwhelming."

"I've been here before, and they are. But they're not insurmountable if you're dedicated. Now, enough of the socializing. I'll assume since you haven't gotten up and walked out yet, you're still in."

"I'm in."

"Good. Where do we start?"

NESTO LAREZA WATCHED Rhonda Amherst leave Cappie's with the well-dressed stranger. The pair got into her SUV, which Amherst then steered out of the parking lot and headed south on Pacific Avenue. Lareza assumed from her direction Amherst was probably headed home, but then he dismissed the idea. He could hardly believe what the sheriff had told him about the captain's involvement with the as yet unnamed killer running around putting holes in any dirt-bag criminal that moved. Not that Lareza could find a reason to be all that broken up about it.

It was the suspicions of his superiors concerning Amherst that had Lareza worried. He could hardly believe his ears as they talked of false arrest, hiding evidence and protecting a person of interest in the recent violence against gangs in Ladera Heights and Culver City. But now, in this moment when he could see her secretive behavior, he had to wonder. It pissed him off he could even think about Amherst in that way. He'd known this woman for years; she'd been more dedicated to her job as a police officer than anyone he knew. He could hardly believe she'd play footsy with the feds without letting her actions be known to the sheriff. And he certainly didn't believe she had any part in the drugs. That was asking him to swallow too much.

No, obviously something else had to be going on, and Lareza planned to find out what. If nothing else, he could stay on Amherst's six and be there to cover her ass if she got in trouble. Somehow he figured the guy accompanying her didn't pose any immediate threat. Amherst had always possessed a knack for sniffing out trouble, and she wouldn't have even let him in the car had she sensed danger.

Lareza had never been able to admit to himself or Amherst how he really felt about her. In any case, he couldn't have ever brought himself to tell Amherst how he felt because he feared rejection. It wasn't an irrational fear, in his mind; they had tried to be more than friends once before without success.

Amherst didn't use the turnoff at Pacific that would have taken her back to the house. Instead, she kept heading north. None of this made sense to Lareza. Where the hell was she going? They passed Montana, continuing onto Wilshire, and then she turned and headed directly for Lincoln. Maybe she had planned to take her visitor back to the airport. Lareza took his eyes from the road long enough to flip open the cover of his cell phone.

He put it to his ear and said, "Downtown." The phone began to dial the number to LASD headquarters and within a minute Lareza had his boss on the horn.

"Sheriff, this is Lareza. I decided to tail Captain Amherst, see for myself if your suspicions are founded. I'm beginning to think they are. She met some suit, looks like maybe a fed, and now they're headed who knows where. Do you want me to stay on her?"

"You're damn right I do," the sheriff replied. "In fact, don't let her out of your sight. I'll send someone to relieve you in a couple of hours once you know their destination."

"I still don't feel overly confident about this, sir."

"I know she's your friend, Lareza, but I'm not sure she can be trusted. You understand duty, son. You understand commitment. That's a hell of a decent trait to have. I wish more cops had it."

"I understand."

"You keep on her, Lareza. Don't give up."

"Yes, sir."

Lareza hung up and smacked his lips at the suddenly sour taste in his mouth. He didn't like this, not one damn bit, and the temptation came over him to either abandon his pursuit or make his presence known to Amherst and her escort. Lareza shook it off. He had to remain strong until he could tell what was actually happening. He still couldn't come to terms with any wrongdoing on Amherst's part. There had to be a better explanation.

And Nesto Lareza planned to find out what.

Bolan scanned the wharf through the night-vision binoculars.

From his vantage point directly across the wide thoroughfare designed for tanker staging and large vehicles, he could take in the view of his first target. The warehouse was dwarfed by its neighboring structures, and there didn't appear to be any activity outside. All the action probably happened inside—the same action that had brought him here. Bolan had one purpose on his mind tonight: destruction.

The more Bolan read Tan's intelligence about the Golden Dragon, the angrier it made him. Police in Jakarta, as well as most of the DEA presence in-country, considered the Dragon responsible for much of the drug trade in the Golden Triangle, and most of that appeared to be heading straight for America.

The time had come to start burning down the operation.

Bolan keyed the throat microphone clipped to his belt. "Jack, sitrep."

"All quiet on the western front," Grimaldi came back. Bolan had stationed the pilot in a rental at one end of the thoroughfare, which enabled the Stony Man pilot to keep an eye on things at ground level. He'd double as the escape mechanism for Bolan and a little bit of backup, too, if necessary.

"Not a creature stirring?"

"The rats," Grimaldi cracked, "but I'll spare you details."

"Thanks. I'm hoping this intelligence from the Bear pays off. I can't believe anything Tan tells me, unfortunately."

"Why's that?"

"He lied to us, Jack. When I asked about drugs coming in from other areas, he dismissed it out of hand. Said it would be competition. We know there's stuff flowing in here from Pakistan, Afghanistan and about a half dozen other countries."

"I see," Grimaldi replied. "And any DEA agent who knows anything about anything would know that."

"Yeah," Bolan said. "I don't think Tan's that stupid. So why lie about it?"

"Maybe it's a territorial thing."

"Maybe, but for now we feed him only need-to-know on our operations here until I can get a better angle on him."

"Understood."

"Time to rock the boat. Be ready."

"Roger that."

Bolan killed the switch on the VOX system, checked his watch and then withdrew a long, slender pipe from a slit pocket in his blacksuit. He unfolded the pipe at a hinge set in the middle, effectively doubling its length. Bolan flipped up a small laser-dot pointer and aimed it at the roof of the warehouse, then slammed his palm against the back of it. The internal plunger struck a blasting cap, and in turn sent a metal rod sailing in a graceful arc across the thoroughfare. Tongs of a vanadium-steel alloy bit into the roof. Bolan tied off the loose end and in one smooth motion he slid down the rope spanning the thoroughfare. He landed almost noiselessly on the warehouse roof.

Bolan activated the VOX system and announced, "I'm down." That would be his last transmission until he was ready for extraction. He didn't want Grimaldi getting too close to the action on this one. The pilot could easily hold his own—no problem there—but the Executioner couldn't be sure what he'd encounter and he wanted an escape route ready if things got too hot.

The Executioner double-checked the action on the Brigadier and MP-5 before heading to the rooftop access door. His suspicions it would be locked were confirmed, but two minutes flat with a lock-pick set granted him entry. Bolan waited just inside the door, allowing his eyes to adjust to the pitch-black stairwell. He decided to make this a soft probe if at all possible. He couldn't be one hundred percent certain he had any better intelligence than Tan, which meant this penetration could result in a total bust. If that was the case, he hardly felt like alienating locals, not to mention blowing away some innocent simply at work.

When his eyes adjusted, Bolan quietly padded down the steps with his back to the wall and the Brigadier held at the high and ready. He'd opted not to make the MP-5 his primary weapon, since an SMG would prove more awkward in close quarters like this. A pistol would be more swift and accurate, and thereby more effective.

Bolan reached the base of the stairs and encountered another door. He turned the handle and it opened easily. He edged it a few inches to make sure it didn't squeak in protest; the seaside air had an accelerated oxidizing effect on metal, and rusty hinges tended to squeak. No sound came from the door.

Bolan slipped through the opening, let the door close behind him with a soft click, then crouched and studied his surroundings. The warehouse seemed poorly lit. The warrior let his eyes scan the surroundings, taking in every detail. Of chief concern would be places where he could lay an ambush as much as where he could be ambushed, as well as alternate routes of escape if he encountered trouble. The clacking of distant machinery seemed to drown out most of the sound, a fact Bolan received with considered gratitude. At least he could move without worrying about his every footstep being heard.

Bolan rose and moved along rows of cardboard boxes stacked high. He maneuvered through the narrow aisles for several minutes, seeing and hearing no one. He soon reached the end of an aisle that opened onto a very wide doorway. Ahead he saw the machinery, which looked like little more than an assembly-line packaging center. The boxes and packaging obviously ended up stored in the back section of the warehouse, because those on the packer were identical to the rows stacked up all around Bolan.

The Executioner cautiously emerged from his position and walked toward the machinery. He got within ten yards before spotting human movement to his left. A small native man sat on a tall stool at one end of the long row of machines, repeatedly tapping his foot on some type of pump beneath the machinery. He would then quickly inspect the line of boxes rolling down a slight incline to his position and occasionally push them off to another set of rollers directly ahead of him, which ran perpendicular to where they came off the assembly line.

Bolan watched this process for several minutes until he saw a small forklift roll into view. The operator expertly got beneath the stack of boxes where they rolled to a halt just beyond the older man's position, lifted them by pallet, then backed up with his stack and disappeared from view. To all appearances, it seemed as if there wasn't a thing out of place. That's what had Bolan so suspicious—everything seemed a little too perfect.

The warrior edged back from view, holstered his pistol and considered his options. The warehouse had people inside who appeared unaware they were part of a front operation. Bolan could hardly believe what he saw, and while he hadn't yet seen proof positive this place served as a front for the Golden Dragon's operations, he could hardly ignore previous failures by Tan and his people. Somebody had managed to feed Tan false information, and further convinced him the Dragon was operating as a mover rather than a shaker.

Bolan knew he shouldn't have allowed himself that moment of distraction, because it nearly cost him his head. Literally. The Executioner neither heard nor saw his would-be assassin, but he'd learned to pay attention to that sixth sense—

the one that caused the hairs to stand on the back of his neck and left a bowling-ball-in-the-gut feeling. Bolan dropped prone in time to avoid having a wire with a pair of sharp blades separate his head from the rest of his body.

Bolan rolled to his left and spun sideways before launching both feet in a kick at his assailant's legs. He caught only a glimpse of the enemy, but enough to set his teeth on edge.

The man had a short, muscular physique, and was dressed completely in black garb save for the stripes of red and gold circling his wrists, ankles and waist. Additionally, he wore a decorative multicolored rope around his forehead as a headband; it stood out in stark contrast to the black mask totally concealing his head and face. The man made no sound as the shank heels of Bolan's combat boots struck his right knee. He twisted away, taking less of the blow directly to the patellar area, and despite the ferocity of Bolan's countermeasure he remained on his feet.

Bolan used the distraction to get to one knee. His attacker attempted to punch him, but the warrior blocked the blow with a forearm and fired a punch of his own, catching his shadowy opponent midsection. Air whooshed from the man's lungs, and Bolan followed up immediately with a leg sweep. The man leaped into the air to escape the maneuver and tried to come down with one foot on Bolan's throat. The big American rolled clear of the foot stomp and regained his feet.

The attacker immediately rushed Bolan, but this time the Executioner was ready. He sidestepped the attack but nearly lost his balance while lashing out a palm to block an elbow strike intended for his ribs. Bolan launched an uppercut from the knees that caught his opponent off guard. The blow lifted the shadowy attacker off his feet and slammed him into one of the rows of stacked boxes. The man slid down and shook his head, trying to clear the obvious cobwebs left by the punch, but Bolan didn't plan to give him time to recover. He whipped the 96 Brigadier Inox from shoulder leather and aimed it center mass.

A rigid forearm suddenly snaked around his neck and immediately cut off oxygenated blood to his brain, while another hand reached out to grab his pistol arm. Bolan knew the move well because he'd executed it many times, and he also knew he had less than ten seconds before his world went black. Bolan jumped once in the air, then hit the ground running backward. At the last moment, he stopped suddenly and dropped to one knee, throwing his upper torso forward simultaneously.

His assailant sailed right over Bolan's head and landed prone on the ground in front of him, arms splayed out. The Executioner took one knee, steadied the pistol in a two-handed Weaver's grip and squeezed the trigger. The first bullet entered the choker's spine just below the neck and continued upward until it lodged in his brain. The first of Bolan's attackers had just gotten to his feet but hadn't found time to do more than that. Bolan ended any further aggression by pumping off a double-tap to the chest.

So much for a soft probe, he thought.

JACK GRIMALDI SAT behind the wheel of the rental and absently watched the warehouse.

Other considerations preyed on Grimaldi's thoughts; at the moment, most of them focused on Sonny Tan. Like Bolan, the Stony Man pilot had learned to read people pretty well, but he hadn't formed any impressions about Tan deceiving them. The guy had seemed willing to help. Still, Grimaldi knew Bolan wouldn't ignore his gut-level instincts and especially not when it came to the state of things in Jakarta. If the nearly legendary stories behind the Golden Dragon held even a grain of truth, Grimaldi knew it wouldn't take the Executioner long to figure it out.

The Stony Man pilot felt his eyes go heavy, but he let his will intrude and overcame any thought of succumbing to his exhaustion. Bolan counted on him, and he'd never let the big guy down before—he sure as hell wouldn't start now. Grimaldi looked at the radio and considered turning it on for moment, but he dismissed the idea quickly. He needed to keep his focus. At that point, he couldn't even be sure why he felt this restlessness. Maybe a lot of it had to do with being cooped up so long. He'd look forward to stretching his legs, maybe soaking up some sun. He felt long overdue for a vacation.

Figures, maybe a half dozen, emerged suddenly from the shadows of the building directly across the thoroughfare from the warehouse Bolan had targeted. They wore black garb that resembled ninja outfits, and black masks concealed their faces. They didn't move like ninjas, though, and those weren't swords they carried. Grimaldi could discern the silhouettes of SMGs even from that distance. The pilot waited until they had crossed the thoroughfare and merged with the shadows of the warehouse before making his move.

Grimaldi started the engine, put the car in gear and gunned it right from second gear. He waited until the vehicle came within about thirty yards of the building, then he hit the headlights. Several of the men were caught off guard, apparently having been oblivious to the sound of the car engine. Grimaldi didn't even slow down. He jerked the wheel hard right and then left, which caught a pair of the unwary gunmen dead to rights. Car metal screeched against the corrugated alloy of the warehouse exterior, and Grimaldi smeared the two hardmen against the wall.

The Stony Man pilot jammed on his brakes and then went EVA, fisting the SIG-Sauer P-239. He stopped neither to kill the engine nor close the door, instead sprinting to the edge of the warehouse. He risked a glance around the corner in time to see three men slip inside and a fourth take up a post at the door.

Grimaldi raised his pistol in a two-handed grip, braced his hands against the corner of the warehouse and squeezed the trigger twice. The first round missed, but the second resulted in a clean head shot that blew the enemy gunner's brains everywhere. Grimaldi gritted his teeth, nodded in satisfaction and then keyed up the VOX.

"Head's up, Sarge," he said in a tight whisper. "You got company."

Silence was the only reply.

AT THE MOMENT Grimaldi's report sounded in his ears, Mack Bolan had his hands full.

Another one of the black-clad assassins seemed to appear out of nowhere and tried to knock the pistol from his grip. He got a slug point-blank to the face for his troubles. Bolan heard a scream and looked up just in time to see a second man leap from a stack of boxes that reached nearly halfway to the roof. The warrior could do little more in the moment than roll clear, a bit surprised by the overwhelming assault.

As he came to his feet, any doubts he had on the accuracy of Stony Man's intelligence were summarily dismissed. There could be no question he'd touched a nerve, and if he managed to pull out of this alive it would certainly raise the stakes for all sides. Bolan snap-aimed the pistol at his latest opponent, but his shot went wild because another assailant managed to catch his blind spot and kick the pistol from his grip. The kicker tried to jump on Bolan and catch him in a headlock, but he came away with a knife to the midsection. The Executioner had managed to clear the blade from his load-bearing harness before his opponent could react.

His adversary rushed him, and Bolan countered with a side-kick that contacted the man's cheek. The black-clad assailant recovered quickly and fired a double punch to Bolan's left kidney. The Executioner clenched his teeth against the pain while sucking air through his nostrils. He spun to his right to protect his unguarded side while simultaneously landing an elbow on the other fighter's chest. The man grunted with pain, but he seemed unhurt.

Bolan took a side stance and dropped low, waiting for the next attack. His opponent stepped back instead of rushing him, and Bolan immediately sensed trouble in the move. Instinct proved him right once again. Three more men had joined their friend, and Bolan had now come face-to-face with four trained assassins. They looked like ninja but they didn't move like them. Bolan had fought Japanese martial artists before, and the dress of these men was where the resemblance ended. No, he'd come up against a far different style this time around.

The man he'd originally been facing off with shouted something unintelligible.

"You going to talk me to death?" Bolan asked him, widening his stance even more to improve his center of gravity.

The man let out another yell, this one in the universal language of rage, then the quartet charged. Bolan blocked the first two blows, but a well-placed kick from one of the men caught him in the temple. The impact sent fiery lances of pain from his temple to the base of his neck, and stars popped in front of his eyes. The Executioner reeled from the vicious assault, threw up his arms. Destiny saved him from a second cruel fate as the move blocked a punch that would have otherwise finished the fight.

Two of them managed to get behind him and pin his arms, and Bolan took a rock-hard blow to the gut, then another. The wind rushed from his lungs, causing his chest to burn and the stars to return. Objects around him took on the appearance of a photographic negative, and blackness all but overtook him.

Bolan waited for the final blow that would bring death, but it didn't come. He willed himself to stay upright, fighting the arms that bound him, but he couldn't seem to make his balance return. He tried to muscle his way free but to no avail. Before he could think to switch tactics, something like an insect sting bit at the nerves in his neck. Bolan tried to slap at it, but his head started to swim more and the consciousness he fought hard to retain just wouldn't come.

Bolan felt the muscles in his face go taut. A smile? Maybe, although it was really of no surprise, because he could hear Grimaldi's voice. That seemed good. He knew his friend would come and back him up. Yet his elation at being rescued didn't last, because he knew he simply couldn't trust what he heard. Barbara Price's voice suddenly followed Grimaldi's, and Kurtzman's booming laugh followed that.

Bolan felt his feet drag across rough ground, the bump-bump-bump repeating thunderously in his head, but he still couldn't seem to control his body. He tried to fight, but his reflexes didn't respond. And then the Executioner remembered he'd experienced this same euphoria a few times before. He'd been drugged.

And water spray in his face, the roar of a boat motor, would not wake him.

Brognola and Amherst realized about the same time they had a tail, but Amherst mentioned it first.

"Yeah, I thought so, too," Brognola replied to her news.

"You're the higher-ranking officer here. How'd you like to work this?"

"That depends," he said. "Where are you taking us?"

"There's a guy I know, an informant. He used to play a major role in the gangland drug trade here until he became a daddy. That cleaned him up and got him out of the gangs altogether. He still has his nose in the business, though, and he'll even part with the information."

"For a price?" Brognola asked as his eyes flicked to the side mirror.

Amherst shook her head. "Not at all. His knowledge acts as an insurance policy more or less now. He keeps quiet about the particulars of certain operations and in return enjoys the 'protection' of the heaviest hitters."

"You mean, organized crime?"

"Yep." Amherst clucked her tongue. "Everybody's in on the heroin market action in Los Angeles. Sometimes even the judges and politicians get a cut. Knowing who's involved is never the problem. It's someone having the means and motivation to cross those individuals. They wield a power and influence like no other criminal element you can imagine."

Bet I could, Brognola thought, but said, "Well, I'm here to change that."

She looked at him and chuckled. "You plan to take on the better part of L.A. County?"

Brognola fixed her with a hard gaze and did nothing to hide the seriousness in his tone. "If we have to."

"We're only a few blocks from this guy's house. I need some options."

"We should—"

That's all Brognola got to say because the roar of glass shards flying through the SUV, followed by a pop and a hiss, drowned him out. The interior filled immediately with smoke. Tear gas! It hadn't come from the rear; someone had obviously driven alongside and fired it through a backseat window. It took all of Brognola's wits not to succumb to the choking miasma of noxious gas. The Stony Man chief tried to roll down his power window but it wouldn't budge. Maybe Amherst had inadvertently engaged the window lock.

The police captain was keeping plenty busy herself. She started to swerve, trying to keep the vehicle in control, but it proved impossible under the circumstances. Amherst slowed to a speed where she could safely steer the SUV off the road. It bounced onto the curb, rolled across the corner of a lawn, taking part of a chain-link fence and child's toy shopping cart with it, and bumped to a stop with the assistance of a telephone pole.

Both occupants bailed immediately. Although his eyes and lungs burned from the prolonged CS exposure, Brognola had enough sense to draw his pistol. He looked for any sign of Amherst, concerned he might mistake her as an enemy, but his watery eyes made seeing next to impossible. He resisted the urge to rub them. The formation of crystals in the tear ducts was a side effect of CS gas; rubbing his eyes would only worsen the condition. Time and fresh air were his best defenses at the moment.

Brognola first heard the threat in the form of tires screeching to a halt on pavement. The big fed grabbed the cover of a thick tree trunk, blinking rapidly to clear his vision. Car doors opened, followed by the whip-crack of automatic-weapons fire. Brognola couldn't see the enemy, but he perceived the pistol shots as return fire. The direction was what puzzled him most. He'd expected to hear only one pistol, the one belonging to Amherst, if any at all. Instead, he heard reports from two distinctly different pistols.

His vision finally cleared enough to give him his first blurry glimpse of the scene. Amherst had sought cover behind the front end of her SUV close to Brognola's position, down on one knee while she white-knuckled her pistol in a two-handed grip. Their tail vehicle occupied a space immediately to the rear of the SUV, and a muscular Latino with short-cropped hair had taken up his own firing position behind it. Brognola got a first look at the opposition. They had arrived in a jalopy van. He counted at least six gunmen, all attired in camouflage fatigue pants and black T-shirts. Chemical protective masks concealed their faces. They were dark-skinned, but not black, which probably meant Spanish or Middle Eastern descent—he bet on the latter.

The SMGs stuttered with renewed vengeance, and Brognola's vision cleared enough that he felt safe returning fire. Innocent bystanders were his biggest concern. Toys were strewed throughout the yard surrounding them. He braced the pistol in both hands, aimed center mass at an exposed enemy gunman and squeezed the trigger twice. The first round caught his target in the chest, and a crimson spray testified to Brognola's marksmanship. The man's muzzle swung skyward as he triggered several rounds reflexively. Brognola's second slug ripped through the gunman's throat and slammed him against the van.

Brognola looked for another target, but the remainder of the gunmen had obviously realized they weren't bulletproof and took cover. It surprised the Stony Man chief their tail had ended up an ally, but it surprised him more when the guy left the safety of his vehicle and ran for Brognola's position. Bullets nipped at the man's heels and chewed up bits of earth, or buzzed past him and just barely missed tender flesh. The guy made it, out of breath but no worse for the wear.

"Just thought I'd let you know I'm on your side," he said.

"I gathered," Brognola replied, cocking one eyebrow. He risked a quick peek from cover and ducked away when a fresh storm of lead threatened to decapitate him. "Why were you following us?"

"Orders," he said.

"Whose?"

"L.A. County sheriff's," he said. "Listen, can we get into that later?"

"Sure." Brognola couldn't help but grin. The guy was much younger—Amherst's age or thereabouts—with dark hair and chiseled features. He possessed intensity. Call it a cop's intuition, but Brognola immediately sensed something good about this guy and decided to trust him. "What's your name?"

"Nesto Lareza. You are?"

"Hal."

"You with the feds?"

Brognola nodded. "How'd you know?"

"The suit," he shot back with a lopsided grin. "The suit *always* gives you away."

"Great. Any ideas on how we get out of this?"

"Help's on the way. I radioed it in as soon as I saw them pull up next to you."

"They fired tear gas through the side window?"

"Yeah, sorry about that," Lareza said. "By the time I realized what was happening, it was too late to do anything about it."

Before either man could say another word, they heard a staccato burst of gunfire followed by a yelp coming from Amherst's direction. Brognola knew that cry—she'd been hit.

He looked once at Lareza and then burst from cover and fired repeatedly, although not indiscriminately, in the direction of the enemy as he rushed toward the SUV's front end. Brognola sensed Lareza on his heels, the cop laying down his own barrage of covering fire. The pair reached Amherst's cover unscathed and found her propped against the bumper, her forearm bleeding profusely.

"Just a bite," she told them through clenched teeth.

Lareza reached into his back pocket and withdrew a red bandana. He immediately dressed her arm and cinched it tight with a knot.

"That should stop the bleeding," he told them. "Now what?"

"How long before the cavalry arrives?" Brognola asked.

The wail of approaching sirens answered his question. They would have to hold off their assailants only a couple of more minutes. Considering what they were up against, those minutes could seem like hours. Their first course of action would be to get back to the cover of the tree, which would provide them with greater cover. Brognola pitched the idea to Lareza, who agreed—until Brognola suggested the cop take Amherst and go first while he provided suppressive fire.

"No way," Lareza said. "We all go together or we don't go at all."

"Listen, we're out of time," Brognola told him. "Now, I'm the senior man here, and I'm telling you this is how we do it. Understood?"

Lareza chewed his lip a few seconds, considered his options and then, realizing he didn't really have any, he nodded. "Okay, sir."

Lareza and Amherst prepared to leave cover and on a three-count they rushed for the tree. A volley of automatic weapons opened up on them, and Brognola returned fire. The Stony Man chief managed to get another assailant by sheer luck. A .45-caliber slug ricocheted off the van and fragments penetrated the eye socket of one of the masks. Blood exploded from the lenses, and the wearer staggered uncertainly before dropping to the ground.

The police units had rounded a corner of the street and were on a fast path toward the van. The remaining shooters stopped their assault and jumped into the vehicle. They peeled from the scene in a concert of smoking tires and burned rubber. Brognola broke cover, along with Lareza and Amherst, who had made it to the tree unscathed, and the trio laid down an impressive hail of gunfire in an attempt to disable the retreating van. One round had to have hit just right because a moment later the van swerved precariously first right, then left. The vehicle's back end fishtailed and abruptly whipped around, causing the tires to strike the curb. The force flipped the vehicle onto its side. Brognola dropped the magazine from his Colt, slammed home a fresh one and fired repeatedly at the exposed undercarriage until rewarded with a gasoline-fueled explosion. Flames and black smoke roiled into the air with a final, violent whoosh of gas fumes released from pressure.

The squad cars screeched to a halt and appeared to spew an army of LAPD officers. They screamed at the trio to drop their weapons. Brognola complied and gestured for his compatriots to do the same. It wouldn't do to have survived this round only to let the cops gun them down. There would be plenty of time to explain themselves and show their credentials once things had calmed. Following that, Brognola planned to pay a visit to Santoso and Hamzah.

First, however, he had some unfinished business with the L.A. County sheriff.

The blinding, skin-burning, mouth-drying experience of returning to consciousness from a drug-induced coma had officially made Mack Bolan's top-ten list of bad experiences.

The Executioner had been drugged before, but never quite like this. The substance his enemies had used had left him with something that felt like a cross between a hangover and post-chemotherapy. Pain, like white-hot needles lancing the backs of his eyeballs, radiated from the center of his head to the tips of his earlobes. His mouth felt as if someone had coated the interior with paint thinner. The muscles in his arms and legs burned with exhaustion, as if he'd been supporting lead weights for hours at a time. In fact, Bolan didn't think there wasn't a spot anywhere on his body that didn't ache, burn or otherwise hurt like hell.

"He's awaking, guru," a smooth, almost melancholy voice said.

While Bolan heard the voice, knew the speaker had made his statement at a normal volume, the words reverberated through his mind. Each syllable had an almost "clacking" quality, like ball bearings striking each other in one of those perpetual-motion machines that sat atop the desks of executives. The warrior didn't know who had spoken or whom he'd spoken to. Had the man said *guru*? Who would have been addressed by that name?

THE NEXT TIME BOLAN woke up his head seemed clearer and a good amount of the pain had dispersed. It felt as if he sat slumped against a cold, metal chair, and a quick rocking of his body confirmed it was bolted to the floor. His hands were bound behind him, causing the muscles in his wrists and forearms to ache. He wiggled his fingers and clenched his fists to help restore circulation.

Bolan could lift his head enough now to make out the shadows that surrounded him. The periphery of his vision still seemed a bit fuzzy, but he couldn't positively attribute it to the darkness versus the drugs. Whichever the case, someone had done his homework on the Executioner's tactics. The only way he could have been taken alive would be if someone drugged him. Why had the enemy gone to such an effort to drug him? Was this the work of the Golden Dragon or some other entity? If the former, why take him alive? If the latter, who would have any personal interests in him?

Bolan began to consider not only the alternatives but also a way to escape. It remained his goal and paramount duty. During wartime as a soldier, the Army had taught Bolan the primary goal of a prisoner *had* to be escape. It remained that way to this day in his mind, although the gathering of intelligence he could use against his enemy bore equal importance. The success or failure of any task rested on a warrior's ability to conduct operations unmolested against his enemy. To risk any further delays would compromise Bolan's mission.

The time to act had come.

Bolan calmed his mind and began to assess his surroundings. First he closed his eyes and slowed his breathing, timing himself to approximately three a minute. Inhale five seconds, hold five seconds, exhale for ten and then repeat. Simultaneously, he tried to extend his auditory senses to the very edges of the room, let them come fully alive so he could listen for breathing, whispered conversation—anything that would help him sense the presence of someone else in the room. After a few minutes of concentration, he opened his eyes in complete satisfaction he was alone.

Bolan tried to move his wrists inside the restraints now that some circulation had returned, but he didn't feel a bit of slack. An expert had obviously tied his bonds, and he didn't believe he'd easily be free of them. He had a better sense of his position now. His captors had definitely tied him to a chair and stretched his legs out and apart, which made it extremely difficult to move in any direction. The Executioner willed his mind and body to relax. He considered his options and concluded the enemy hadn't left him many.

Bolan's senses went into high gear at the sound of a door opening, followed immediately by a cultured male voice. "Ah, you are truly awake this time. Too bad the guru had to step out. He did not want to miss this opportunity."

Bolan thought about replying but recanted the idea. Maybe his host would continue chattering aimlessly until he revealed some little tidbit the warrior could use to make his escape.

"Oh, the strong and silent type," the voice continued. "Excellent. That will make the challenge all that much sweeter for me. And the guru, of course. Yes, we must wait for him to return."

Lights came on everywhere suddenly and nearly blinded the unprepared Bolan. Before his eyes could adjust to the harsh glare, a hand came out of nowhere and slapped him hard across the face. The blow threatened to dislodge teeth and caused Bolan to bite the inside of his cheek. He tasted the immediate saltiness of his blood, smelled the ironlike scent, and as the sting of the slap wore down he could sense the blood trickle down the side of his lip. There was little he could do about it. He tried to contain the blood, swallow it in pure stubbornness, but the angle of his head and body caused him to nearly choke on the puddle forming in his cheek.

Bolan spit out the blood and stared daggers at his captor. The man stood no higher than five and a half feet if he stood an inch. Shocks of unkempt black hair protruded from his head like stalagmites—it looked almost as if someone had glued it to his scalp in patches. He had a light complexion that stood out starkly against the dark hair and eyes. But his most prepossessing feature was the smell of destruction and death. Bolan knew the scent all too well, and it practically emanated like a field of energy from this man.

"My name is Jarot Pane. You might wonder why I struck you." He walked behind Bolan and bent. Bolan felt Pane's hot breath on his earlobe. "It's to remind you *I'm* in charge here. Every bad thing you experience is because of me, and every good thing, including relief from any pain or discomfort, is also at my whim."

The man stood and returned to his previous spot, where he faced Bolan. "That is the way of things. There can be no good without bad, no light without darkness."

Bolan didn't put stock in those words nearly as much as he did the sudden flash of pain in his palm as he adjusted his hands, trying to work out some of the numbness that had returned. Bolan expressed impassivity, tried not to react to the stabbing pain, but only a few seconds elapsed before he felt the hot tickle of blood running down the outside edge of his left thumb. A metallic sliver protruded from the back leg of the chair, its edge sharp enough to cut Bolan's thick, callused hand.

"Would you agree?" Pane rambled.

"Whatever you say," the Executioner replied.

Pane folded his arms, and his smile gave his face the same appearance as that of a blanched skull. "I see you're as stubborn as the guru warned us you would be. That is good. It should make your, ah, inquest look all the more interesting."

Inquest? Bolan hadn't heard that word in a couple dozen years, and he wondered where Pane had been educated. The guy surely had that much going for him. His speech and mannerisms betrayed the classic training he'd received from who knew where. It came as a surprise to Bolan that the Golden Dragon would let someone of Pane's intellect serve as his lackey. He hadn't considered the Dragon to be all that bright based on Sonny Tan's description. There had to be more to it than that. Bolan considered the possibility of a homosexual relationship but quickly dismissed it. These kinds of men were men's men—or at least they liked to make outsiders think as much.

Bolan saw the blow coming this time and managed to turn his cheek in time to take about half its intended force.

Pane chuckled as he reached down and grabbed Bolan's hair from the top of his head and pulled straight up. "Your reflexes are excellent. Excellent. You will, indeed. make a fine subject for interrogation. However, I do not want to use you up just yet."

Pane released Bolan and turned, oblivious to the ice-cold blue eyes boring into his back like invisible javelins. Bolan thought about playing his card right then, but he knew it wouldn't do much good until he could figure out where they had taken him and what kind of resistance he could expect to meet on his way out. One thing remained certain, though.

Before this mission ended, the Executioner would kill Jarot Pane.

ANGER AND FEAR GRIPPED Jack Grimaldi—anger at not reaching Bolan in time, and fear of what the captors would do to his friend. The fact they had chosen to take the Executioner versus leaving his dead body to be found gave the Stony Man pilot reason to hope Bolan remained among the living. He didn't hesitate to tell Price and Kurtzman as much via the encrypted satellite phone every member of Stony Man carried.

"Any idea who took him?" Price inquired. "Or why?"

"You know as much as I do," Grimaldi replied. "The majority of Sarge's intelligence is based on what you guys gave him."

"There is that," Kurtzman said.

"What about Tan?" Price asked. "You think he could help?"

"I don't know that Sarge trusted Tan all that much," Grimaldi said. "And frankly I've learned to trust his instincts on things like that. Still, I'm going to play it cool for now and ask for his help. Way I see it, we need to solicit all the cooperation we can right now if there's any hope of getting Sarge back breathing and in one piece."

"I can have Phoenix Force airborne in an hour, if need be."

"I appreciate that, but you know Sarge doesn't like to involve them unless it's absolutely necessary. We've been here before. And by the time they get here, if I haven't found him by then I may not, at least not alive. This first twelve hours will be critical." Grimaldi paused and allowed himself a smile even though his friends couldn't see it. "Besides, you know how grumpy David McCarter gets if I'm not at the stick."

The pilot heard Price sigh. "Okay, it's your call since Striker's out of commission and Hal's in L.A."

"What's he doing there?"

"Following up with Amherst," she replied.

That got Grimaldi thinking. "Really? That's interesting."

"It looks like there may be more to this than drugs," Price added.

"I think Sarge figured something like that from almost the beginning."

"Well, Hal got suspicious when Striker said there didn't appear to be any connections between the drugs and any of the major gangs in the area known to deal in that kind of weight. It begs the question that if the major dealers on the receiving end didn't even know the drugs were being distributed through their territories, then who did? And why didn't the gangs do anything about it?"

"I get it," Grimaldi interjected. "And it does make it look like there was someone else behind the whole thing. When Sarge mentioned something about the Golden Dragon's acting as purely distributor, Tan sort of pooh-poohed the idea saying he didn't think a guy like that would risk such a low profit angle."

"But you're thinking the Dragon might risk it for a bigger payday," Price concluded. "Something we hadn't thought of before now?"

"Right."

"Okay, so let's suppose you're right. How else could someone benefit from flooding the market with drugs but not be all that concerned about profit margin?" Price asked.

A long silence followed. It was clear nobody had any real answers to that question. The best thing they could do at that point would be to pass the theory onto Brognola and see if he could come up with anything. It was Grimaldi who finally suggested it, and Price and Kurtzman had little choice but to agree with him.

"One way or another, we'll get to the bottom of it," Price finally said.

"I'll get back with you as soon as I finish talking to Tan."

"Be careful out there, Ace," Kurtzman said.

"Will do. Out here."

Grimaldi disconnected the call and then gave his full attention to the road. Traffic had become thicker in the uptown area. Only one major artery led in and out of northern Jakarta, and at the moment cars, buses and trucks clogged its lanes. There wouldn't be any easy way to negotiating the traffic, and the fact many buildings were crammed together proved Grimaldi's only mercy in the end game. The pilot reached Tan's headquarters in under thirty minutes.

The place occupied a cramped, first-floor suite in a six-story building with a primer-gray panel facade and a cheap purple awning outside a single door covered with wrought iron bars. The interior smelled of dust and disuse. Travel posters adorned the walls, and a pair of angled desks occupied the center of the room. A petite, dark-haired native studied Grimaldi with deep brown eyes. She seemed innocent enough, even cheap from a certain point of view, but Grimaldi's trained eyes spotted plenty of the intelligence mixed with suspicion behind those dark orbs.

"Yes, sir," she said. She had an accent, but Grimaldi couldn't place its origin. "How may I help you?"

"I'm here to see Mr. Tan."

"Um, Mr. who?" She shook her head and smiled sweetly. "I am sorry but I do not know—"

"It's okay, Lanana," a voice interrupted.

Grimaldi turned to see Sonny Tan had entered the room. Except for the Asian lines in his face, the guy looked like he'd come straight out of a *Miami Vice* episode. He wore white slacks accompanied by a skintight, powder-blue shirt and silvery, sheen jacket. Grimaldi could barely see the hint of a pistol riding in shoulder leather.

"I need to talk to you," Grimaldi said. "Right now."

Tan jerked his head in the direction of a doorway, and Grimaldi followed him through it. They entered an area twice as large as the front office. The walls consisted of maroon wainscoting that rose to waist height and then merged with mahogany red paneling. A stove and refrigerator occupied one area, a door led into a single bathroom in another corner and a third area had been sectioned off into a pair of makeshift bedrooms with metal cots and bedside tables. A wall mount supported a small TV-VCR combo and rose above a three-seat couch. A dark-haired guy in jeans, flower-pattern silk shirt and holstered Glock pistol lay on the couch snoring softly.

"How quaint," the Stony Man pilot remarked after taking it in. He directed a sideways glance at Tan. "I can see your accommodations are up to the usual government standards."

"You'd call it bare-bones living," Tan replied with a shrug. He gestured in the direction of his snoring companion and added, "We call it home."

Tan kicked the bottom of the man's shoe and he came awake with a snort. In most cases it would have been nothing short of suicide to wake up an armed member of Stony Man's teams like that, but over here things appeared a bit more lax. Grimaldi could understand it. Many agents in the DEA these days complained that outside of the U.S. they could contribute very little to the war on drugs. Most of this was due in part to apathy on the part of governments in those countries because they simply didn't have the time or resources to combat drug exports. They were too busy fighting health epidemics, local crime, hunger and poverty.

Grimaldi knew the ills of the world; he just didn't know how to cure them. It seemed so much had transpired over the years. He'd followed the Executioner through one hellhole after another, and there were moments where the pilot wondered if it was all worth it. After all, what had they really contributed to this fight? Sure, they'd done a whole lot of good, saved a whole bunch of lives, but in the end who outside of their own little group had given a tinker's damn? And in the big picture, had they really made a dent in the empire of Animal Man?

Kill the philosophy, Jack, he told himself. *You're here to help your friend.*

"Get up, Sleeping Beauty," Tan said.

The guy grumbled awake, rubbed his face with his hand, then came to a sitting position and smacked the inside of his mouth. "What the hell you waking me up for?"

Tan jerked a thumb at Grimaldi. "This is Jack, guy I told you about. He's working with Cooper." Tan suddenly stopped and whirled to face Grimaldi. "Where *is* Cooper?"

"Somebody snatched him," Grimaldi said. "That's why I'm here. I need your help to find him."

"When you say *somebody,* what exactly does that mean?" Tan's partner asked in a thick Scottish accent.

Tan gestured at him. "This is my partner, Felix Tobridge."

Tobridge nodded. "Pleasure."

Grimaldi returned the nod and said, "These guys were…I don't know, ninjas or something. They didn't look Japanese but they were sure dressed like them. They wore these black *gi's* with red-and-gold stripes, and they had hoods on. They were fast and strong, but fortunately they weren't bulletproof.

They ambushed Cooper, almost like they'd been waiting for him. I need to know if you know who they are and how they operate. Anything you can tell me would help."

Grimaldi stopped a moment to take a breath. He realized he'd been rambling.

"Holy shit," Tobridge said, "those sound like *pechin*."

"Come again?" Grimaldi asked.

"*Pechin*," Tan said, confirming Grimaldi heard correctly the first time. "They're an ancient order from the Ryukyu samurai class of Okinawa."

"That's why they were dressed similar to ninja," Tobridge added.

"Well, where can we find them?" Grimaldi asked.

"That's going to be tough," Tan said with a sigh. "Rumor has it they work for the Golden Dragon as enforcers. We won't find them unless we find the Golden Dragon."

"Or unless they find us," Tobridge said, climbing from the deep cushions and coming to his feet. "If they saw you, they know you're affiliated with Cooper. That means when they're done with him, they'll come for you next."

"Or they'll try," Grimaldi said. The offer Price had made to send Phoenix Force was beginning to look better and better to him by the second.

"I've got an idea," he said. "I wonder if we could get them to come out of the woodwork again."

Tan smiled. "You figure if we draw them out, make some kind of sucker play, it'll eventually offer us an opportunity to follow them back to their lair."

"Exactly! Maybe they'll lead us straight to Cooper and the Golden Dragon."

"It just might work," Tobridge said. He looked at Grimaldi. "The question is, how do we draw them out? You're not dealing with stupid people here."

"He's right," Tan said. "The Dragon is said to be one crafty son of a bitch. How do you figure on playing this?"

"Well, you've said the Golden Dragon's got control of the entire market here in the city, right?"

"Sure."

"You know any places where you can get his product in sufficient quantities?"

"What type of quantities?"

"Enough that if it suddenly went missing that would draw the Dragon's attention?"

Tan shrugged. "Maybe. But how's that going to help draw out the *pechin?*"

"Because they'll never tolerate someone taking what belongs to them," Grimaldi replied.

Hal Brognola seethed as he waited outside the door with a plate mounted on it reading: Hon. Dominic Hanford, Appellate Court—District 3.

He chewed constantly on an unlit cigar and paced the hall located in the Los Angeles Federal Building. Brognola ran down his options at this point in the game, and each time his instincts ticked off another choice on the list for some arguably sound reason. Brognola wasn't any more accustomed to making rash decisions than being made to wait on others. In the big picture, he could have resolved the entire situation with a phone call, but he considered it poor form to get the President involved with these kinds of situations simply for the sake of expediting what he perceived as bureaucratic red tape.

Finally out of patience, Brognola whirled and charged through the closed door of Hanford's chambers. He caught the judge by complete surprise, as well as a pair of suits seated across from him. Brognola gave the pair only a cursory inspection and immediately read them as federal agents of some kind. It took him only another moment to recognize Howard Starkey and Bart Wikert.

Brognola ripped the sopped stogie from his mouth and said, "You two, out!"

All three men jumped to their feet. Wikert opened his mouth to speak, but Brognola didn't give him a chance.

"I don't know what the hell you're doing here," Brognola

said. "You were both ordered to stay out of this. Apparently, your hearing isn't so good. So get the hell out of here!"

"Now, just a minute, Mr. Brognola," Hanford said. "They're not done."

"Oh, yes, they are, Judge," Brognola replied with a bit more respect. "I'm sorry to barge in, but time's short and I far outrank this pair. They have no jurisdiction here."

The judge hardly made for an imposing presence, standing maybe five foot nine and weighing in at 185 pounds. A row of thin hair surrounded a dry and flaky bald spot. Reading glasses rode low on Hanford's pug nose, and anger mixed with surprise brought a flush to his ruddy complexion. Brognola considered just how inconsequential Hanford looked as he put his hands on his wide hips.

"And I suppose you do?" Hanford demanded.

"My jurisdiction is the United States and her protectorates," Brognola said. He jerked his thumb at Wikert and Starkey. "As I'm sure these men can attest."

Hanford stared at Brognola a minute longer and then looked at the pair. "Is this true? *Were* you ordered off this case by him?"

"Yes, Judge, but not by him," Starkey said.

"Actually, he's not in our direct chain of command, Your Honor," Wikert added.

"I'm in everyone's chain of command, pal," Brognola said. He reached into his pocket and withdrew his cellular phone. "You want to call and check it out? Dial your supervisor now. Tell him Harold Brognola's here, and I've caught you with your hand in the cookie jar again. See what he has to say."

A long silence followed, and neither man moved to take the phone from Brognola. The Stony Man chief nodded, harrumphed and then stuck the phone back in his pocket. Wikert and Starkey looked to the judge for help, but it appeared they no longer had Hanford's attention. The men made a not-so-graceful exit, and Brognola closed Hanford's chamber door after them.

Brognola consciously slowed his breathing some before speaking. "Sorry for the dramatics, Your Honor, but this is important and I can't afford to wait any longer. Those two clowns have already disobeyed direct orders once and nearly cost the life of another federal agent, not to mention a local police captain. I meant no disrespect."

The judge studied him a moment, then gestured to one of the seats, again taking his own leather office chair. "I'll overlook it this time, Mr. Brognola. Next time, however, why don't you simply try knocking?"

"Of course," Brognola said. He cleared his throat and continued, "I need your help, Judge. I need a warrant to take charge of two criminals currently under the custody of local law enforcement."

"Who, exactly?" Hanford asked.

"The Los Angeles County Sheriff," Brognola replied.

With that, the Stony Man chief began to recount the details of the events over the past forty-eight hours, save any reference to Bolan or his activities. He disclosed information on the capture of Maki Santoso and Shihab Hamzah, and identified their involvement with the drug trade in the Golden Triangle's underworld, not to mention Hamzah's known affiliation with the JI.

"You make a strong case, Brognola," Hanford finally declared. He pulled a pen from the holder on his desk as Brognola reached into his coat and withdrew the federal order. As he signed, Hanford said, "I'll grant you full and unconditional custody of these two men pending a complete and thoough investigation into their activities. Under the *Homeland Security Act* you have seventy-two hours before you are required to provide either proof of their involvement in a terrorist plot or you *must* permit them to seek representation."

"And what about their current attorney, Your Honor?" Brognola asked. "Will they be allowed to retain him?"

"Are either of the men American citizens?"

"No, sir, they're both here illegally as far as I know."

"Then they're not entitled to representation under Miranda or otherwise," Hanford said with a shrug.

Brognola smiled and Hanford smiled back as he handed over the warrant. "Bring these bastards down, Mr. Brognola."

"Count on it, Judge."

ARMED WITH A WARRANT, Brognola's next stop was Amherst's house. She'd taken Brognola back to the parking lot at Cappie's Lounge where he picked up his car, then went home to clean up while he returned to the airport, changed clothes and picked up the warrant. Amherst looked refreshed as she climbed into the sedan and Brognola—having caught a few winks himself—put the sedan in gear and headed for the North County Correctional Facility in Castaic.

"How did it go?" she asked.

"Like clockwork," Brognola replied, grinning.

"Mind if I ask you something?"

"Shoot."

"Why did you bother to go through all these hoops just to obtain a warrant? Seems to me you could have handled this by making a simple phone call."

"You think so, huh?" He shrugged and continued, "You're probably right, but the fact is the agency I work with is walking on political eggshells. Some people very high up believe we've outlived our usefulness."

"If you're the only ones around to stand up against a crew like the one this morning, I could hardly believe that," Amherst said.

"Thanks for the vote of confidence."

"What's the plan?"

"We'll start by taking a large bite out of Hamzah and Santoso," Brognola said. He patted the breast pocket of his coat. "With this warrant, they're now in federal custody for official purposes of the Justice Department. We'll find out what they're up to."

"Yeah, that warrant puzzles me a little," she ventured. "I'm not sure why you even needed it."

"Look, if I go through unofficial channels to get things done, I'm going to draw unnecessary attention. We've already done enough of that, and I don't want to do anything that might spook the enemy. Our best bet is to play it cool and see if we can draw them into the open."

"Well, they've already tried to kill us twice, so I say it's a pretty good guess you're on the right track."

"Those were only hired guns," Brognola said. "I'm more interested in finding out who's behind the whole thing. This isn't about drugs anymore, Captain. I don't think it ever was. This is about something bigger, and we need to find out exactly what that 'bigger' is."

"Is that why Cooper ran off to God knows where?"

"That's why," Brognola said with a nod.

They reached the jail within twenty minutes and found Nesto Lareza, attired in full uniform, waiting in the parking lot for them. He shook Brognola's hand in a very formal fashion, then squeezed Amherst's hand and gave her a quick hug. His face said it all, he had bad news.

"What is it?" Amherst asked.

"They wouldn't wait any longer," he said. "They let them go."

"The prisoners?"

Lareza nodded.

"Who let them go?" Brognola asked.

"Sheriff."

"I've about had enough of this guy," Brognola said. "Come on."

The big fed walked through the parking lot and straight into the vestibule of the North County Correctional Facility. While smaller than many of the other detention facilities in L.A. County, the bleach-white building was nearly twice as wide as tall; a large bow window stretched above the main entrance. Central-air units hummed quietly under the shuffle of people's feet and waiting visitors.

Brognola inquired into the sheriff's whereabouts and within a few minutes, a uniformed detention officer escorted him to a side office. The place wasn't terribly big but Brognola wouldn't have called it cramped, either. He felt no discomfort in the fact the sheriff had agreed to see him alone. Apparently, whatever was going on he didn't wish to explain his actions in front of subordinates. He could decide not to tell Brognola anything, and there wouldn't be much the Stony Man chief could do about it. After all, he didn't have any warrants forcing the sheriff to talk to him.

The door to the office suddenly opened to admit a tall, distinguished-looking man with thinning gray hair and a salt-and-pepper mustache. He possessed an aura of command that reminded Brognola a lot of Mack Bolan.

"Brognola? I'm Sheriff Maxwell Garner. Thank you very much for waiting. I'm up to my eyeballs in work today."

"No problem," Brognola said, careful not to come off as adversarial. "I know what you mean. I have a lot of those days. Seems they come more and more as you get older."

Garner smiled as he sat behind his desk. "Isn't that the truth? So, what can I do for you?"

"I'll try to be succinct, since I'm sure your time's limited," Brognola said. "In short, you authorized the release of two men this morning. These men are suspected of terrorist acts."

"I know exactly who you're talking about, and unfortunately I have to disagree," the sheriff said. "You see, I think you've made some kind of mistake here."

"Oh, really?"

"Yeah," Garner replied, never dropping his smile even a moment, as if it were chiseled into his face. "Mr. Santoso is gainfully employed by Leonard Weste. You know the name?"

"The big movie mogul," Brognola recited from memory.

"He's more than that. He's a top-rated producer and agent in Hollywood. Very influential man…very close friends with the governor, I might add. He also knows the mayor and probably a dozen or more of the most powerful political entities in this state. He also happens to be a personal friend. I can personally vouch for Mr. Weste, and for anyone in his employ."

"And that includes Santoso?"

"Yes, sir."

Brognola smiled. "Sheriff, would it surprise you at all to learn that Maki Santoso is a native of Indonesia and a known criminal wanted by authorities in Jakarta for at least a half-dozen felonies?"

"I would say you don't have your facts straight, Mr. Brognola."

"Would you?" Brognola sat back, crossed his legs and folded his arms. "How do you explain Mr. Santoso being discovered on Raul Montavo's yacht?"

"That's very easy to explain," Garner replied. He stood and cracked the window in his office, then fished into his shirt pocket and withdrew a pack of cigarettes. He offered one to Brognola, who declined, then stuck one between his lips and fired up. "Filthy habit, I know. Wife keeps nagging me to give it up. Plus, not really supposed to smoke in here although pretty much everyone turns a blind eye." He winked. "I guess there's a benefit or two to being the L.A. County sheriff."

"I would imagine," Brognola replied with a placating smile. "But I would like to get back to my original question—"

"What's that, huh?" Garner looked as if he hadn't really been paying attention, but he waved at Brognola. "Oh, yeah, back to Maki Santoso. You were asking about him being on the boat. Mr. Weste actually owns that boat."

"But it's registered to Montavo," Brognola said.

"Mr. Weste owned him, too."

"So he's found dead on it with six other people," Brognola replied, not missing a beat. "And by the way, he happened to be in Jakarta just a few weeks ago. And we both know one of the deceased was Kara Lipinski, daughter of an influential politician who probably got his elbows rubbed by Weste. Are you seeing the same pattern I am, Sheriff?"

"Mr. Brognola, Santoso was on that boat looking for something," Garner said easily. "Those two men had my authorization to go on that boat."

"That boat was an unprocessed crime scene," Brognola countered. "Why would you authorize such a thing? A favor?"

"You could call it that," he said. "And those men weren't supposed to be unescorted. Someone dropped the ball."

"Yes, and that someone was you, Sheriff. Whether you believe Santoso's a crook or not doesn't really matter. What does matter is that you also let his friend go, Shihab Hamzah. A quick check through NCIC would have flagged him as a known member of the Jemaah Islamiyah. In case you're not aware of it, the United States declared the JI a terrorist organization quite a number of years ago, and they're still very much pushing for a fundamentalist Islamic theocracy throughout all of Southeast Asia."

"What's with the history lesson, Brognola?" Garner's tone had taken an edge now.

"Not history, geography. Indonesia is part of Southeast Asia, and so is Myanmar, the largest distributor of heroin and opium to the United States. The same heroin and opium you asked Captain Amherst to keep quiet about."

"Yes, I understand she's with you," Sheriff Garner said, "despite the fact I placed her on administrative leave pending an investigation that may result in criminal charges."

"I don't think so," Brognola said. "She's operating under my protection now."

"All due respect, Mr. Brognola, but you don't have any jurisdiction over her or the LAPD, for that matter. Sergeant Lareza is on loan to my agency by approval of his unit commander, and I'm the law in this county."

Brognola decided it was time to play his hand. He reached beneath his coat and withdrew the warrant. "This is a federal order granting me custody of those two men under citations in both the *Patriot* and *Homeland Security* acts. That gives me jurisdiction where they're concerned. It also gives me whatever authority I need to pursue and detain these men. They are now considered fugitives of the U.S. government."

Brognola got out of his chair, dropped the copy of the warrant on Garner's desk, turned and headed for the door. When he reached it, he said, "Captain Amherst and Sergeant Lareza are now under my command, Sheriff. If you have a problem with that, call the deputy director of Homeland Security. He'll confirm what I've just told you. And before this is over, don't be surprised if it's you facing charges."

And with that, Brognola walked out and returned to the foyer where Amherst and Lareza waited patiently.

"What happened?" Amherst asked.

"You were right," he said to Lareza. "He let them go."

"Why?" Lareza asked.

Brognola shook his head. "Never mind that now. And congratulations, by the way."

"For what?"

"You just joined the Justice Department," he replied. "You're now deputized U.S. marshals."

"Awesome!" Lareza said with unabashed enthusiasm.

Amherst deadpanned, "Great. Just what I've always wanted."

Brognola turned and led them from the NCCF. When they reached the parking lot, he said, "Our first order of business is to find our two fugitives."

"That may not be easy," Amherst said. "It's possible they've already left the country."

"I would have agreed with you an hour ago," Brognola replied. "But now, I don't think so. I don't think they can leave."

"Why not?" Lareza asked.

"There's something pretty big going down. Garner sort of gave away their game plan when he told me both Santoso and Hamzah are employees of Leonard Weste."

"Whoa," Amherst interjected. "Heavy hitter, that one."

"Don't interrupt," Brognola said. "I'd bet they've gone back to Weste, and I think Garner knows it. That means it won't be difficult to find them, but it's going to get very difficult to apprehend them."

"Do you think the sheriff's part of this whole thing?" Amherst asked.

"I wish I knew," Brognola said. "Even if he is, I can't prove it so it doesn't make much difference. Unfortunately, I'm afraid I probably alienated him in our little meeting. That means we can expect no support from that part of law enforcement. Beside the fact, I don't think the locals have the resources. And after our little run-in with that team this morning, I think it's time we call in some additional resources."

Even as he said it, Brognola wished he had the Executioner there now to consult. Not just because Bolan would have known what to do but because he really could have used a friend right at the moment. He knew Amherst and Lareza would stick by him, but he couldn't be sure how equipped they were to handle the situation. Phoenix Force was out of the question for a mission like this, and Able Team was tied up with another crisis. For now, it would be up to him to hold down things on the home front until Bolan could return.

He thought of Bolan and wondered what the soldier might be into right at that moment.

Mack Bolan had cut his hands at least four or five times during the course of trying to free them from the ropes, and his right hand was bleeding freely. The sudden release he experienced when he did get through the ropes took him a little by surprise after the grueling hours of sawing at the thick fibers using only the strength in his forearms, and in an awkward position at that.

His hands now free, Bolan retrieved the small pocketknife tucked in a pouch on the inside of his combat boot and cut away the ropes that bound his feet. His fingers and toes immediately tingled—the skin grew hot as the circulation fully returned to them—but Bolan moved past the sensations and kept focused on the task at hand.

Pane had darkened the lights again, and that gave Bolan the advantage. The room had no windows, so he couldn't tell if it was day or night. He hoped too much time hadn't elapsed. The clock ticked and the numbers ran down as each minute passed. If he didn't determine the location of the Golden Dragon and shut down his operations soon, the whole country would be flooded with more pure-drug product than it would know what to do with.

Bolan wouldn't let that happen.

The warrior used his pocketknife to cut away the inside fabric of a slit pocket in his blacksuit and bound his bleeding right hand with the makeshift bandage. He slipped the knife into a spring-loaded carrier under his right sleeve, then searched the room for anything he could use as, or convert to, a weapon. He found nothing, which gave him pause to consider his options. The knife wouldn't be enough to get him out of there if his opponents were well armed, and Bolan suspected they were.

Undaunted, Bolan went to the door and pressed his ear to it. He gently tested the handle, then turned it. The lock mechanism moved freely and without a sound; Bolan's enemy had fortunately relied solely on his bonds to hold him captive. The Executioner would make sure it proved their undoing.

Bolan pulled at the door. At first it seemed stuck, but a second and more forceful tug freed it from the doorjamb. Light spilled through the crack, and Bolan let his eyes adjust a bit before peering through to a stark, undecorated space with a few tall plants and small trees scattered throughout the room. Bolan saw no guards and no surveillance cameras. He eased the door open a little more and slipped between it and the doorway. He closed it quietly behind him and crouched. No angry shouts or alarms resounded. The room remained tomb quiet.

The Executioner took a moment to consider his options. He spotted two doors leading from the room. One was recessed into the same wall as the one from which he emerged, which left Bolan to assume it was nothing more than a similar room to the one he'd occupied. The other door stood in the wall directly opposite that one, and looked identical to the other pair. For a moment, Bolan considered the possibility he might be walking into a trap. Jarot Pane did seem sadistic enough to pull one of the oldest tricks in the book. Make a prisoner feel as if he had a chance to escape, give him the opportunity to taste freedom, then spring a trap and drag him back to his cell.

Bolan shook it off. When he considered the fact he didn't have many other options at this point, it couldn't hurt to give it a try. Maybe fate would deal some favored cards into his hands that would allow him to turn the tables on Pane, if the man even had such a plan in the works. The first favored card reached Bolan about halfway across the room when the light reflected off something running across the floor.

Bolan, who had been proceeding toward the door with extreme caution, stopped and knelt. He put his face close to the floor and exhaled; his breath frosted over something thin and taut—a trip wire. Bolan moved along its length to the wall and after careful inspection he spotted the very small holes patched with circular disks of something that had much the same makeup as rice paper.

Bolan moved his forearm and the pocketknife sprang into his right hand. He whipped out the blade and cut carefully around the edges until he'd exposed the hole. The fierce edge of a dart peered back at him. Bolan carefully extracted it for inspection. Close scrutiny revealed something reddish brown and sticky coating the tip: drugs or poison?

Either one didn't matter, because Bolan would not trip the thing. On a whim, he extracted a few more of the darts, sheathed his knife and pocketed them. Keeping his back to the wall, Bolan then relocated the wire where it joined the wall and stepped over it. He continued along the perimeter, more careful to assess for additional traps. Eventually he reached the door without incident.

Bolan turned the handle and pushed. The door swung wide-open.

"LOOKS LIKE WE MIGHT'VE found the place, guy," Felix Tobridge announced.

Grimaldi lifted the binoculars and studied the exterior of the large building as a sleek black Mercedes-Benz parked in front of the entrance. Two men in suits and sunglasses emerged from the vehicle and immediately disappeared inside. The building occupied a section in the red-light district, but it seemed like the last place the proud *pechin* would operate. Still, that kind of stereotype could very well be one of the reasons the Golden Dragon and his band of thugs had operated unmolested for so long.

Mack Bolan had taught Grimaldi long ago never to take things at face value.

Grimaldi studied the building a bit longer. Most of the windows were dark with tinting, the front entrance fairly nondescript. Grimaldi fidgeted a bit, wishing for one of those fine Cuban cigars in which he occasionally indulged, and finally procured the last stick of gum from the pack he'd opened that morning.

After planning their ruse for this place based on a thorough review of Tan's intelligence, Grimaldi and Tobridge prepped their equipment while Tan went to run down some additional leads. He should have been back at that point, but so far he hadn't shown. Grimaldi wondered if the guy would make it. Tan's insistence he gather new intelligence in the midst of trying to trick the *pechin* into leading them to Bolan's whereabouts smacked a little bit of a stall tactic. Still, he'd left instructions to proceed without him if he didn't make it back on time, and that said something for his desire not to impede the search for Bolan.

Grimaldi lowered the binoculars and checked his watch again for about the tenth time in a row. Only a few minutes remained until H-hour, and still they hadn't seen or heard from Sonny Tan. A three-burst squelch suddenly issued from Tobridge's radio and interrupted Grimaldi's musings. Tobridge grabbed it from the seat between them and keyed the handset.

"Go ahead," he said.

"I'm back," replied Tan's voice, recognizable even through the poor reception and electronic modulation. "You guys set?"

"Yeah, we're good and ready," Tobridge said. He looked at Grimaldi and added with a cocksure grin, "Although I think our newfound friend here is getting edgy."

"I show two minutes to showdown," Tan said.

"Acknowledged," Tobridge replied, and then he dropped the radio onto the seat.

Grimaldi snatched it up quickly and keyed the talk button. "Remember, don't move in until you get my signal."

A single squelch burst in return indicated a yes; two bursts would have indicated a change that required discussion. Grimaldi replaced the radio and lifted the binoculars to his eyes once more.

As the pilot studied their target, Tobridge spoke up. "Sonny knows what he's doing, you know. You can trust him, mate."

"I know," Grimaldi said, although he didn't hear any conviction in his own voice, which meant an observant guy like Tobridge wouldn't, either.

"You don't sound like it," Tobridge pressed.

"Listen, I can understand your loyalty to him, okay?" Grimaldi replied. "But you've known him a long time, and I haven't. And you should be able to understand my first loyalties are with Cooper. Okay?"

"Fair enough," Tobridge said. "But understand that Sonny's saved my life a couple of times. We look out for each other. We spend about every waking moment together, which means three years of holidays, American *and* Scottish, and other special occasions. Buddy, I'm telling you he's family to me, and that makes him one hundred percent reliable in my book."

"Glad to hear it," Grimaldi said. He lowered the binoculars, looked at his watch once more and then said, "Let's go."

The two men went EVA and walked toward the building very nonchalantly. They couldn't be sure what kind of real resistance they might encounter, so the plan would be to keep any and all weapons out of sight until absolutely necessary. And then, it would only be if someone tried to make hard contact first. Grimaldi and Tobridge crossed the street and walked along the sidewalk parallel to the building.

As they drew closer, Tobridge said casually, "Looks like a club."

Grimaldi only nodded. They approached, forty yards, thirty, and finally they were within the ten-yard mark. The

Stony Man pilot knew that distance to be significant because most shootings took place at about seven yards or less. The sidewalk looked clear—the sedan had left and turned the corner—but as they reached the entrance a trio of muscle-bound hardmen appeared and stood in their path.

Grimaldi, who'd been sauntering along with hands in pockets, stopped abruptly and looked up at the lead man towering over him. "Hi."

"What do *you* want?" the man asked in heavily accented English.

"Just taking a walk," he said, backing up a step and almost leaning into Tobridge.

"Take a walk somewhere else," the big man rumbled.

The Scot stood taller than Grimaldi. He put his arm around the Stony Man pilot. That hadn't been part of their ruse, to act as a gay couple. Damn it, why the hell had Tobridge decided to improvise? If they got out of this unscathed, he'd be certain to kick the Scot's tail for deviating from the game plan without consulting his teammates first.

"What's the problem here?" he demanded of the leader.

"I told you to find another sidewalk," the big man replied. "And you'll do it if you know what's good for you."

Tobridge nodded, then dropped to one knee, pulling Grimaldi with him. The leader's brows furrowed as he watched them drop, followed a millisecond later by the eruption of blood and gray matter from his skull. The pair standing behind him was disoriented by the spray, and Grimaldi felt Tobridge shove him away before he saw the DEA agent's hand rocket to his jacket and withdraw his Glock. Tobridge took careful aim and blew away both of the remaining goons before they could recover. One's head exploded in similar fashion to that of his boss, while the second took two lung-crushers to the center chest. Both men hit the ground, one of them coughing and retching blood as he died.

Grimaldi started to open his mouth in anger against Tobridge when the guy's chest suddenly exploded. Hot crimson spewed in every direction, and blood from tearing of the aorta by a high-velocity bullet spurted from the wound with each contraction of his heart. Grimaldi looked for the shooter only a moment, then remembered discretion would be the better part of valor. He scrambled like a crab to the awning stretched across the entrance and then sought the cover of the vestibule. Grimaldi drew his pistol and prepared to defend what precarious position he had.

The rage lumped in his throat as he realized he'd been deceived.

MACK BOLAN FOUND the view into the adjoining room much less friendly than the one in which he currently stood.

Five of the ninja-style warriors were scattered throughout, and all of them immediately looked in his direction with surprise. A level of recognition might have been due for their instantaneous reactions had they exercised any forethought before just rushing Bolan. The Executioner had been up against them before, and he knew how they operated. To attempt to defend against them as a whole had proved his undoing the first time around; this time he'd divide and conquer.

A flick of his wrist and tightening of forearm muscles landed the knife handle in his fist. Bolan whipped out the blade just as the first pair of his opponents made contact. The warrior shifted his weight and executed a sliding movement that left him out of their line of attack. The attackers ran straight into each other with a skull-cracking sound that rendered them both instantly unconscious. Bolan caught a third guy on his shoulders by driving his knife into and up about the level of his enemy's solar plexus. Blood squirted onto Bolan's already blood-soaked bandage, even staining some of the sleeve of his blacksuit. As Bolan yanked the knife free, the man issued a grunt of surprise mixed with pain, then his body hit the slick wooden floor.

The Executioner felt a hand drop onto his shoulder, and he reacted instantly with an elbow strike to the ribs. Bolan went high with a second elbow strike as he pivoted into the movement, catching his opponent with a skull-numbing blow to the temple. The man's eyes seemed to vibrate in their sockets. It served as enough distraction for Bolan to finish the job. He planted the point of the knife under the man's chin, driving it upward with enough force to go through the soft tissue and tongue, and ultimately penetrating the upper palate. Bolan shoved the man away, oblivious to the man's reaction at the shock of having his lower jaw pinned to the upper.

Bolan whirled to face his final opponent with the sound of shots echoing in the grand open room; it distracted both of them as they searched wildly for the source. Bolan could see the front entrance of the building. Time stood still a moment as he witnessed three bulls in suits fall under the cacophony of reports, followed a moment later by Grimaldi scrambling up to the doors on hands and feet, coming to rest with his back to the plate glass.

A new sense of urgency welled up in Bolan's gut, and he executed a snap-kick to his opponent's groin. The man barely managed to block the street-savvy move, but he deflected it enough that it contacted his thigh. The killer launched a short punch intended to crack Bolan's jaw, but the Executioner dodged the blow and parried with a forearm block. The two circled each other like samurai titans in a bygone age, each searching out an advantage over the other.

Bolan stopped circling suddenly and went for a double-leg takedown. His opponent bought the feint, and too late he realized his mistake. Bolan changed direction at the last moment, spun on his heel and landed a knife-hand strike against the vertebral prominence that marked the seventh bone in the spine. The hardened shell turned to mush under Bolan's strength. His opponent screamed with anguish and collapsed under legs that no longer worked. His breathing got shallow as he lay prone on the burnished wooden floor—with his spinal cord injured at that level, nothing below his nipple line would work.

Bolan would have finished it, rendering the man a merciful kill rather than leaving him paralyzed, but his friend took precedence at that moment. The warrior rushed to the doors, kicked one open, reached out and hauled the surprised pilot indoors. The pair barely evaded the bullets that ripped through the awning, tearing through it like tissue paper.

Grimaldi gripped his friend's shoulders, and cried, "Damn, Sarge, you're one hell of a sight for sore eyes!"

"Ditto," Bolan said. "What's going on?"

"I'm not real sure, but I think your suspicions about Tan may be correct," Grimaldi replied.

Bolan nodded. "We'll get into that later. You get any chance to study the layout of this place?"

"Plenty."

"Figure a back way out of here?"

Grimaldi nodded. "I memorized actual floor plans. There's a back exit on the second floor. Some steps lead from it to an alley."

"You got wheels?"

"Yeah, but they're out front."

"We'll have to double back, then," the Executioner said. "After you, Jack."

Grimaldi took point and led Bolan to an elevator. They ascended to the second floor and exited onto a long hallway. They traversed the corridor in a flat run and at the last door on their left Grimaldi tried the handle. Bolan could tell immediately it wouldn't budge. He eased his friend aside, stepped back and put his foot against it six inches below the lock. The door gave violently and swung open to reveal a dark, dusty room stacked floor-to-ceiling with covered furniture.

Bolan navigated their way through the maze of chairs, couches and end tables along with a slew of cardboard boxes with ink stampings. The pair eventually reached a back door. After a nod from Grimaldi, Bolan put his foot to this one, and it gave a bit easier. The pair emerged onto a grated metal catwalk with stairs, just as Grimaldi promised. They quickly descended to ground level and ran the length of the alley that would bring them out on the side of the building that would be blind to any observers.

Grimaldi coerced Bolan to stop and rest once they had circled the far end of the block. The pilot wheezed to catch his breath, and Bolan couldn't resist a smile and a gibe. "Not as spry as we once were."

The pilot grinned. "Hey, I've kept up with *you* all these years."

"True," Bolan admitted. He looked around them, scanning for watchers, but nothing caught his eye. "How far to circle around and get back to your car? Ten minutes?"

"Sounds right," Grimaldi replied with a nod.

"Good deal. As soon as we get out of here, I want to find Sonny Tan and ask some questions."

"I think you could be right about him."

"Who gave you this location?" Bolan asked, already knowing where the conversation was headed.

"He did," Grimaldi replied. "Set up the whole thing, as a matter of fact."

"Figures," Bolan replied. He rubbed his wrist, trying to ease the inflamed nerves that resulted from various cuts.

"You're hurt," Grimaldi said, expressing concern.

"Scratches," Bolan said. "Nothing a good med kit won't be able to handle. A tetanus shot probably wouldn't hurt, either."

Grimaldi nodded. "There's a hospital close to Tan's office. How's that for convenient?"

"Fine, because he's going to need one," the Executioner replied.

15

Jarot Pane stood before the Golden Dragon on trembling knees. He had allowed a sworn enemy to escape from right under their noses, not to mention the Golden Dragon's identity had been unquestionably compromised. It wasn't like Pane to disobey orders, and that disturbed Sonny Tan quite a bit. The drug lord couldn't understand why a man with Pane's background and education would repeatedly demonstrate such flagrant incompetence.

Whatever the reasons, Tan wouldn't be able to tolerate it much longer.

In a number of ways, the incident at the old brothel had been rather unfortunate. Tan would never have admitted it openly, but he'd grown fond of Felix Tobridge. Killing the man had been a last resort, but he needed to salvage what little he could from their operation. Soon they would have to leave for the United States—much sooner, in fact, than had been in his original plans.

As Tan sat in his chambers and awaited the arrival of his guest, his conviction on success of their plans wavered some. Tan slowly inhaled the aromatic smoke comprised of incense mixed a touch of opium and marijuana; he tried to push the thoughts from his mind through a breathing exercise he'd seen the *pechin* warriors perform during their meditation times. Still, the doubts would not recede. At first the proposal of his colleagues had seemed preposterous.

They presented the plan this way: flood the U.S. drug

market with so much heroin and opium that distributors would not be able to handle it all. This would cause them to make mistakes that would draw the attention of federal agencies. If resources were realigned to deal with a massive threat, a new drug war so to speak, then the Jemaah Islamiyah could accomplish its goals by launching attacks against members of U.S. federal agencies. It would be a jihad like none ever seen before, and it would culminate in the very denigrated and polluted streets these Americans were trying to protect. While he wouldn't have called the plan ingenious, Tan had seen the profit potential for himself. With his connections in the underground drug market in Jakarta—a major transshipment lane for drugs coming from as far as Afghanistan, Pakistan and Myanmar—he stood to make a pretty penny.

Tan had also managed to recruit an army of practically mindless zombies who thought him to be the reincarnated founder of ancient, Indonesian mysticism. Using the historical religious principles of a half-dozen belief systems—Zen Buddhism, Zoroastrianism, Islam and even Scientology—he built a cult of devoted religious fanatics. Given his profile as a DEA agent, Tan knew he wouldn't get away with the charade long. Thus was born the legend of the Golden Dragon, the tale of an enigmatic nobody who wielded irreproachable wisdom and power. The Golden Dragon could control the minds of anyone he chose; the Golden Dragon declared the real from the unreal, as if he'd spoken the very world into existence; the Golden Dragon maintained an air of infallibility and mystery. It had been a cool gig while it lasted, but now the play was up and he had mere days, perhaps only hours, to implement his plan. And now as if he didn't have enough to do, Tan would have Cooper the soldier and Jack the pilot biting at his heels.

"I don't even think I'll ask you to explain," Tan said to Pane. "I'm sure you wouldn't be able to conjure an excuse sufficient to placate me."

"I am sorry, guru," Pane replied with a bow.

"You're always sorry, goddamn it!" Tan snarled. Pane jumped at the uncharacteristically violent reaction. "I have done nothing but my best to teach you in the hope you'd acquire at least a bit of wisdom! I can see I've wasted it like mud on swine!"

Tan stabbed a finger into Pane's chest. "You have failed me time and time and time again, and I've tolerated it! But now I'm out of patience, and so you can consider this your last warning! If you don't pull your head out of your ass, I'm going to seriously fuck you up! I give the order, and the *pechin* will separate your head from your body!"

Tan could see the stinging impact of his words on Pane, because the man began to shake. He'd never spoken to Pane in this way; in fact, he'd never spoken to any of his people with such veracity. But he'd grown quite tired of Pane's repeated failures and inability to complete even the simplest tasks, and he couldn't afford to not see this through to absolute victory. Anything less would be unacceptable, and then *his* life would be forfeit to his benefactors and they would cut off *his* head. The Afghans and Pakistanis were not known for mercy.

Tan snapped at his tunic to straighten it out and then cleared his voice. Quietly, he said, "I want you to get to the plane and ensure all is ready. I have an idea on how we might make good on our plans without bungling this further, or generating greater risk to ourselves than may be absolutely necessary."

"We are leaving?" Pane asked.

Tan nodded. "I must go back to America and oversee the final stages of our plan. *Personally.* I do not trust that dolt Weste. He's already almost compromised the mission through his indiscretion and paranoia, sending those criminal lackeys of his back to Montavo's boat to make sure they couldn't connect him with anything. I do not want to see the same mistake repeated."

"I understand, guru. I shall go immediately." Pane turned to leave, and on afterthought asked, "Should I, ah, prepare our alternate means in case of any more interference by the Americans?"

"There's no need to worry about them," Tan replied. "I've taken care of that little problem for good. Now, get going, as our time is running short."

THE EXECUTIONER COULD describe his enemy in one word: crafty. That meant fate had dealt him cards for a second chance, but there wouldn't probably be a third. Bolan planned to make the most of the opportunity, and he couldn't waste any time. Once they got back to the car and away from the red-light district, Bolan took the wheel and headed straight for Ihza Neechop's residence.

"We're going to need a resupply of weapons," Bolan told the pilot. "It's too risky going back to the hotel for the ones I left there. Tan will probably have the place watched."

Grimaldi chuckled and jerked his thumb toward the backseat where Bolan spotted the bag he'd taken from Neechop. "You wouldn't happen to mean *those* weapons you left, would you?"

"Nice job," Bolan said. "They still got the Beretta and the MP-5, though, so that only leaves the shotgun. We'll have to at least pick up a couple of SMGs."

"Sounds good," Grimaldi said, adding, "You know I'd follow you anywhere, Sarge."

"I hear a *but* coming," Bolan said with a sideways glance.

"It's just I still don't know what makes you think Tan's our man," Grimaldi replied.

"First, he too easily dismissed our theory of the Golden Dragon acting as a pipeline," Bolan replied. "Any DEA agent with his years of experience would have given some weight to the idea. Jakarta's never been much as a major supply center, but its ports and maritime operations make it the perfect distribution funnel. Tan's suggestion the Golden Dragon couldn't make any money off that was absurd."

"I'd never thought of that."

"Plus, let's add his cockamamy story about Montavo's extravagant behavior here in Jakarta. All the evidence I found on Montavo's yacht leads me to conclude he was somewhat of a loner. Not surprising, either, since Hollywood types are usually trying to minimize attention in their private lives. There was a single photograph of a Latin man in the master cabin, a real Rico Suave type."

"You think they were more than friends," Grimaldi interjected.

"I'd guess it was his lover, yeah."

"So if that's true, he wouldn't have had such an infatuation with Kara Lipinski."

"Right," Bolan said. "And he also wouldn't have had any reason to bring her on this trip except to make a showing as Hollywood's Latino lover boy. The other problem with Tan's story is Lipinski's presence here. I had Bear get into the security databases of all inbound authority agencies for Jakarta. You noticed the airport officer who scanned both our passports when we came in."

"Yeah."

"Lipinski was never checked into the country, either through airport customs or the Indonesian port authority. Tan claims his people tailed them to restaurants and tourist sites, and yet there weren't that many charges on Montavo's credit card. And why stay in a hotel? They had a perfectly good yacht. Doesn't make sense."

"So for all intents and purposes Lipinski was never here," Grimaldi concluded matter-of-factly.

"Right."

"Nice work, Sarge. You'd make a great P.I. Maybe you missed your calling."

Bolan grinned. "I doubt that."

IT TOOK NEECHOP only a few minutes to gather the arms and munitions Bolan required, and soon he and Grimaldi were headed for Tan's offices. This time, Grimaldi took the wheel while Bolan did a final check on the weapons. He slammed a magazine home on the MP-5K A-5, a shortened version of the MP-5, and set it on the seat within easy reach of Grimaldi.

"Only 15-round magazines there, Jack," Bolan told him. "Don't spend it all in one place." He passed two additional magazines to Grimaldi to pocket, then turned to his own weapons.

Bolan had acquired one of the only remaining SMGs in Neechop's arsenal, at least any he considered reliable, an HK-53. While similar to one of Bolan's favorite weapons, the Belgium-made FNC, the HK-53 didn't quite meet the specs necessary to be called a full assault rifle. Still, its 5.56 mm high-velocity slugs delivered a big wallop in a smaller package. Combined with the SPAS-12 shotgun in the bag, it would prove an adequate arsenal for whatever Tan might try to throw at them.

He had apparently decided to start with helpless, screeching women because a dark-haired beauty burst from the front door of Tan's offices as the pair exited the sedan. Bolan and Grimaldi took up cover positions behind the door, the Executioner holding the HK-53 at the ready while Grimaldi snatched the MP-5K A-5 from the seat and put the weapon in battery.

The men who followed the woman were dressed as *pechin*, with one minor change—they toted Ingram MAC-10s. The *pechin* spread out at the sight of Bolan and Grimaldi and raised their weapons, prepared to deliver the first salvo of destruction. The Americans beat them to the punch.

The Executioner took the first target with two shots to the chest. Blood and wet flesh erupted and left gaps around the man's sternum. He staggered a few steps, never having reached his cover, before falling prone to the pavement. Bolan caught a second gunner with a short burst that stitched the enemy from crotch to throat. The impact of high-velocity rounds drove the man backward, his arms windmilling as he reeled from the onslaught. The building wall finally stopped him in his tracks and he slid to the ground, leaving a gory mess in his wake.

Grimaldi triggered a 3-round burst from his MP-5K A-5 while he braced the weapon against the crook of the door and A-frame post to steady it. All of the rounds would have scored, but his target moved before Grimaldi could adjust his sights. One bullet managed to land, biting through the man's arm and distracting him. Grimaldi followed up with another 3-round burst that took the guy down as he shouted in pain from his initial wound. One round managed to enter his open mouth and blow out the back of his skull. It cut short the man's outburst.

Grimaldi looked for another target of opportunity but quickly ducked behind cover when the enemy sent their own volley of lead his way. Grimaldi avoided having his head blown off. He heard the tink-tink of the bullets as they perforated the metal of the sedan door, and the buzz of those scorching air overhead.

Bolan saw the heavy fire directed toward his friend and decided to put a stop to it. He broke cover and launched himself in the direction of the threesome who had managed to gain a bit of high ground by climbing into the bed of a pickup truck. Bolan's movements immediately drew their attention from the Stony Man pilot, which was exactly what he'd planned. They turned the muzzles of their weapon in his direction and prepared to target their man.

They realized their mistake just a moment too late.

The Executioner had secured a position that brought him parallel to the truck, and low enough to have a clear shot at the underbelly. Bolan unleashed a full-auto salvo that ripped the guts of the undercarriage, including the gas tank. As precious oil and gas spilled from the truck, Bolan kept up the salvo and then rolled to a new cover position behind a large brick base supporting a light pole. Bits of concrete flew from the sidewalk around him and pelted his exposed skin. Bolan suffered a few minor scrapes but nothing in comparison to those aboard the truck.

The vehicle exploded violently and without warning as the sparks from the autofire ignited the fuel. The truck came off its tires, the heat instantly melting the rubber, and it blew apart. Bolan watched bodies, one intact and the other two torsos, sail over his head and crash against the building. A bloody, fiery mess of flaming clothing and burned flesh rained on Bolan's area of operations, and he had to keep still a minute to ensure most of the most dangerous debris had settled.

Bolan peered around the corner and prepared for another defense, but no threat greeted them. Passersby and cars had immediately maintained a safe distance when the shooting started, and now the explosion would only reinforce their belief that remained the most logical course of action. Bolan also knew it would bring the police very quickly.

"Let's get inside!" Bolan hollered at Grimaldi, jerking his head in the direction of the building entrance.

Grimaldi nodded, got to his feet and immediately sprinted for the front door of the building. The pilot burst into the offices, the Executioner following on his heels. But they were too late. The place had deserted written all over it.

"We only have a minute or two before police arrive," Bolan said. "I'd suggest we use that time to gather intelligence."

Grimaldi nodded and headed for the computer he'd seen in the back room while Bolan rifled through desk drawers and filing cabinets. Bolan had nearly completed his search when Grimaldi called him. It took the warrior a minute, but he found the ace pilot in a small alcove secreted into the wall in such a way as to make it invisible to the average observer.

Grimaldi sat in front of a computer screen that displayed row upon row of database records. Bolan looked over the pilot's shoulder and squinted to make out the electronic print on the small screen. It consisted of ships departing Indonesia and China, all with destination points in the U.S. It included dates and times, with final ports scattered mostly along the California shores.

"This looks like records of the ships that were carrying drugs into the States," Grimaldi said.

"It's more than that," Bolan retorted. "It's a list of *every* ship going into the U.S. I'd hazard a guess and say not all of them were used in the smuggling operation."

"But even if twenty-five or thirty percent got through, that would still make for a large pipeline."

Bolan nodded. "Yeah, and more than enough to be profitable for Tan."

"Why wouldn't his having this information send up some sort of red flag for someone?" Grimaldi asked.

"He's in the DEA. There wouldn't be any reason for someone to question his access to this information."

"Ha... Yeah, guess you're right. It's the perfect cover. This way, he could monitor the shipments without raising anyone's suspicion."

It disgusted Bolan whenever he thought about people who were supposed to stand incorruptible instead sowing seeds of corruption. While those individuals profited the rest of society paid the price, and oftentimes with their very lives. The Executioner had made it his single purpose in life to eradicate those kinds of predators, and Sonny Tan had just added himself to that list without even knowing it.

"Is that thing connected to a laptop?" Bolan asked.

"Yeah, actually, it is."

"All right, let's disconnect it and take it with us." Bolan looked at his watch. "We're out of time."

After ten minutes of getting the third degree from guards concealed behind the steel framework mesh of an intercom and security cameras, Hal Brognola managed to gain entrance to the property of Leonard Weste.

The Stony Man chief shook his head as he steered along a winding drive that led to the estate mansion. Tall green trees swayed in the California breezes amid a landscape featuring luscious gardens that seemed to have erupted from the ground in a rainbow of colors. The water alone needed to keep the place looking like that had to cost a small fortune, not to mention the expansive lawns as fertile and well maintained as any golf course Brognola had ever played on. The entire grounds were a testament to Weste's amassed fortune.

Not that money was something of a scarcity in Hollywood. While the prosperity and stature of the city were wildly exaggerated, some of the grandeur seemed rather understated to Brognola. Most of the influential people in West Hollywood got where they were by one of two methods: birthright or good fortune. Weste fell into the latter category. He'd started as a grip on some go-nowhere, low-profile production, but quickly gained notoriety among his peers for his knowledge and intuition in the film industry. After correctly predicting the success of a film for a big-time distribution executive at Paramount—a venture that ultimately elevated the executive to fame and fortune—Weste came on as personal assistant to the producer at Tantamount Studios, which quickly faced bankruptcy mere months after its inception. Through shrewd investments and license acquisitions on specific projects nobody else wanted to touch, Weste quickly rose through the ranks and took Tantamount to the top with him. Eight years later, the studio signs outside sported a new name: Weste-Tantamount Capital.

Many had taken to calling Leonard Weste the Second King of Hollywood, although nobody had ever bothered to ask who the first had been. It didn't really matter, since Weste now owned most of the town, and it was hard to get a picture made without his stamp of approval, irrespective of what studio actually had the reins of the thing. In short, Brognola brushed up on the guy's dossier before paying him a visit, and according to current Hollywood lore *everybody* answered to Leonard Weste.

Brognola parked his car in front and a valet came to whisk it away. The Stony Man chief shook his head and gruffly said, "Leave it right where it is."

"But, sir, Mr. Weste insists—"

Brognola whipped out his DOJ credentials and flashed the badge. "I said leave it."

The kid, really barely a young man yet, just lowered his head and nodded. He stepped aside and gestured Brognola toward the door. The big fed ascended the low-rise steps and yanked the thick gold cord outside the residence. He could hear the gong of the doorbell as it echoed through the interior of the house, and a moment later a middle-aged man in a tuxedo answered the door accompanied by two of the biggest guys Brognola had ever seen. They also were attired in tuxedos.

Brognola could hardly believe his eyes, because the man who had opened the door required a second look before he could be certain. Brognola let his moment of indecision pass when he realized his imagination wasn't playing tricks on him. He found himself staring into the eyes of none other than Leonard Weste. The movie mogul stood about Brognola's height with a build to match. His clear blue eyes suggested an easier, more cultured life. He wore his white hair with remnants of blond highlights cut close and neat, and a disarming smile accompanied the tan complexion.

"You seem surprised, Mr. Brognola," Weste said in a voice as smooth as fine bourbon.

"Not at all, sir," Brognola replied.

"Of course not," Weste said. "Why would it surprise a policeman that a man of my character would actually bother to dirty his hands by answering his own door?"

When Brognola didn't say anything in way of reply, Weste stepped aside and waved him in. "Please, come in and make yourself at home."

Brognola stepped inside and reached into his coat, just slowly enough that Weste's bodyguards didn't get nervous. He withdrew the federal order and handed it to Weste. One of the bodyguards intercepted the warrant, opened it, made a cursory inspection of the document and then passed it on to Weste with a nod.

"That is a warrant sworn out by a federal judge. It gives me permission to enter any residence and sanctions any operations necessary to apprehend Shihab Hamzah and Maki Santoso."

Weste took the warrant, made the same perfunctory inspection and then passed it back to Brognola. He then turned on his heel, put his hands behind his back and strolled away from Brognola. The Stony Man chief decided to follow, and neither of Weste's bodyguards appeared to make a move that would interfere with him. Weste had complete confidence in the protection offered by both the two men accompanying him and the laws of due process.

"That's all very interesting, Mr. Brognola," Weste finally said. "And I do apologize for my dress and the fact I cannot offer you more than a few minutes, but I have a very important engagement."

They passed through a wide hallway off the main foyer and into a courtyard in the center of the mansion. Brognola looked up to see light streaming through the fog of mist sprayers running the circumference of the open-air rotunda. They kept the area reasonably cool, and provided more than adequate moisture for the plants and flowers spread throughout the vast courtyard.

Weste sat in a chair at one of the several tables and offered one to Brognola, who politely declined.

Weste continued, "You see, the governor's having a party this evening and, well, you can understand I don't wish to be late. He *is* the governor of California, after all."

"Of course," Brognola said. "And I can promise this won't take long."

"Oh, I'm sure. But I must admit I'm a bit puzzled why you've come to me. This is all very intriguing, and I'm sure there are many things you're probably not at liberty to discuss, but I fail to see what any of this has to do with me."

"Really?" Brognola replied with a frosty smile. "Because I've been led to believe that Santoso and Hamzah are in your employ."

Something dark and dangerous entered into Weste's expression, and Brognola mentally prepared for whatever came next.

"I have more than ten thousand people who work for me, Mr. Brognola," Weste said. "But very few of them work directly for me."

"I'm sure that's true, sir," Brognola said, "but I have it on a very reliable word that these two men do work for you *directly,* and that you just recently retained an army of attorneys to insure their safe departure from police custody."

"And just who, may I ask, gave you this 'reliable word,' as you call it?"

"L.A. County Sheriff Maxwell Garner," Brognola said.

Weste didn't so much as fidget in his seat or bat an eyelash, and Brognola knew at that point his plan had worked. Weste had probably figured Garner would keep his mouth shut, not bringing Weste's name into it at all, but he'd miscalculated. If Garner was involved in any illegal activity, he wouldn't take the heat for it, and he sure as hell wouldn't go down alone if he did. He'd drag Weste, Santoso and Hamzah to a federal lockup with him, and it didn't matter who knew whom or what power might be lurking behind the real plot here.

"I do know these men, yes. But I can assure you I didn't know they had been in jail. And since I didn't know that I can say with certainty I could not, and would not, have sent any legal counsel to represent them. I'm afraid Sheriff Garner is mistaken. You have apparently been given bad information." Weste stood and brushed at some imaginary dust on his coat sleeve. "And now, Mr. Brognola, I'm very afraid I must cut our visit short."

"I suppose that means you're not going to give me permission to search these premises," Brognola said.

Weste smiled. "I will be happy to have my men escort you through the grounds and you are most welcome to search where you like. You will not find them here, however. And you can be sure I will report your actions to the highest authority. Now, if you'll excuse me."

Weste turned and headed for a hallway on the opposite end of the courtyard. Brognola watched him go, escorted by one of the bodyguards. He stood there a minute and decided if he should at least make a show of searching the grounds or skip it altogether. He opted not to bother, almost sure Weste had told the truth about Santoso and Hamzah not being anywhere on the premises. They wouldn't have been stupid enough to return here.

Brognola turned to the remaining bodyguard and grinned. "Thanks for the warm reception. I'm sure I can show myself out."

THIS WHOLE OPERATION HAD Maki Santoso ready to jump out of his skin.

Santoso had once led the most powerful underground narcotics pipeline in Jakarta. He'd commanded the respect of more than two dozen lesser drug czars, and rumors of his ruthlessness were the stuff of lore among law enforcement. For years he'd controlled the distribution funnel in Jakarta and surrounding areas with the iron fist of absolute power. Then the Golden Dragon came along three years ago and changed all that.

The Dragon, aka Sonny Tan, swept through the city of Jakarta in a few months and eliminated all of the competition. Santoso found he was able to move right into the operations in the aftermath. At first, he thought he'd discovered a sweet deal; let someone else do the work while he moseyed in and collected the profits. Then he found out that's what Tan had expected him to do right from the beginning. Tan waited until Santoso had taken over the operations, thinning his own ranks without realizing he had a true enemy in Tan. By the time Tan pounced, Santoso realized it was too late and he watched helplessly as Tan swooped in and stole the entire operation out from under him.

As the stories of Santoso's fame died, replaced by the legend of the Golden Dragon, Santoso realized it would be better to cut his losses. He approached Tan with a proposition. Since the police wanted him for a list of crimes that would surely result in death, Santoso proposed a swift and silent departure from Jakarta in trade for his life. He would keep away from any and all pipeline operations in Jakarta if Tan could assure him safe passage off the islands. His employment by Leonard Weste, "a personal friend of the Dragon's," had been the result of that agreement.

All had been going well for the past few years. But as all things that go well for any length of time, it didn't last. Raul Montavo, with his uncontrollable urges for male companionship and insatiable taste in opium, heroin and blackjack, had burned one too many of most of the main suppliers in Los Angeles. That's when he did something stupid and exposed Weste, and that's when Santoso and Hamzah—like all good employees—tried to cover Montavo's tracks so it wouldn't lead back to the old man.

Unfortunately, they hadn't picked the best time to hit Montavo's yacht, attacking him just a mere five miles off the coast of Marina del Rey and bribing certain key players to dock a boat full of bodies and drugs with no questions asked. The police had acted on an anonymous tip, and Santoso had assured Mr. Weste there wouldn't be any questions. They had done everything necessary to make it look like a drug deal gone bad. It wasn't until after the raid that Santoso and Hamzah realized they had forgotten to remove any evidence connecting Montavo to Leonard Weste under a recent deal that hadn't yet gone public.

Weste had wielded his influence on Max Garner to gain entry on Montavo's yacht and ensure they removed the evidence. Instead, they encountered the big dude with the cold blue eyes who had laid them out like nobody's business. The very thought of the guy caused Santoso to shudder, and bringing him up to Shihab Hamzah later during their incarceration hadn't been met with pleasant results.

"If you ever mention this man to me again, I'll kill you," Hamzah had said.

So Maki Santoso tried to forget about that, and concentrate on getting them out of jail. The good-looking LASD captain had almost made it worth the ride, although he couldn't stand the idea of her lies that it was *she* who'd captured them. Still, to discuss the mysterious operator on the yacht was ill-advised, because it would inevitably lead to further scrutiny. They decided it better to keep the man's presence undisclosed until they knew whom they were actually dealing with.

Now Santoso and Hamzah sat and waited in a dusty, deserted house—the only remaining structure in an abandoned movie lot—seventy miles west of the Yuma. Santoso had preferred to leave the state, maybe even the country entirely, but Weste had cautioned against it, pointing out federal authorities would have every mode of public transportation under surveillance once they learned of the pair's release.

Santoso tossed his magazine against the far wall of their makeshift hideout. "This is a cluster-fuck! What the hell are we doing here sitting on our asses? We should be out there finding this bastard and putting a bullet in his head."

"Relax, friend," Hamzah said. "I have worked against men like this before. My people will be here soon. I hear the Dragon's even coming along to personally supervise the operations."

"What operations?" Santoso let out a scoffing laugh. "This whole thing is pathetic. The JI doesn't actually think it can go up against an army of this country's federal agents and win, does it?"

Hamzah opened his dark brown eyes and studied Santoso from his position of meditation on the floor. Hamzah subscribed to all of the religious beliefs of his people. He prayed toward Mecca five times a day, read the Koran with unfailing devotion and committed himself to abstain from tobacco, alcohol and all other vices of the Western Satan. Moreover, he didn't believe in sex but for the purposes of procreation, and he'd applied some additional constraints as a demonstration of his complete devotion to Allah and Mohammed. He didn't dress in the traditional garments of his faith—preferring to lessen the likelihood of racial profiling or drawing attention of law enforcement—but his muscular physique was evident in the short-sleeve shirt and the blue jeans he wore.

"It is not important we win as much as that we make the desired statement," Hamzah said. "My people have suffered under the thumb of government apathy for too long already.

Rest assured, we will succeed in our plans. Whether Tan or Weste profit from the operation is irrelevant."

"Irrelevant, eh?" Santoso thought about this a moment and then burst into laughter. He climbed from the deep sofa where he'd been sitting, crossed the room and got a cold beer from the refrigerator. They had no working television or radio in the house, and it was a mere act of nameless gods that the refrigerator still worked.

Santoso wedged the bottle top against the metal handle of a nearby stove and popped the cap free with a quick downward motion of his palm. He pulled thirstily from it, smacked his lips and let out a sigh of refreshment. "Damn good, this stuff. So anyway, you think Tan and Weste will find lost money irrelevant? That's a joke, Hamzah. If you play with these guys, they'll cut the throats of you and your friends."

"I do not fear them," Hamzah countered. "And you shouldn't, either. It is more important to fear Allah, who has the power to cast not just our bodies away to the great abyss but also our souls."

"Yeah, yeah, you've preached all that doom and gloom to me before. Like I said, I'm not buying whatever it is you're selling. Too many people have already been suckered into that religious shit Tan has been feeding them about the Golden Dragon. Now you think I should bow down to this Allah, or whatever god it is you serve. No, thanks. You can keep that shit because I've already got enough problems of my own."

Santoso returned to the couch and took another long pull from his beer. While he'd been born to a U.S. Marine at a hospital in Jakarta, Santoso wasn't considered an American citizen—at least not by Indonesian law—primarily because his mother had been Indonesian. He was an American in the official sense, sure, but the Indonesian government claimed him, as well, which gave him the dubious honor of dual citizenship by the mere location of his birth. As such, Santoso could enter and leave the country as freely as he could the United States. It had proved quite advantageous on more than one occasion when he encountered problems in America. And since there hadn't been extradition laws between the two countries prior to the year 2001, Santoso had enjoyed what he liked to call "a special sort of diplomatic immunity" during his days as a drug runner.

When it all fell apart, Tan ensured Santoso's adherence to their deal by fingering him for a couple of murders to authorities in Jakarta, and manufacturing evidence to corroborate the accusation. Tan's machinations forced Santoso to leave under dire circumstances and with the full knowledge that if he returned, his adopted country would surely try to execute him.

"If Tan's on his way here," Santoso said reflectively, "that means we'll be able to blow this place soon."

Hamzah nodded. "You have reached a crossroad in your life today with that realization, my friend."

"What?" Santoso sat up and looked Hamzah in the eye. "What the fuck are you yakking about now?"

Hamzah smiled again. "I have worked beside you for two years now, and I have watched your loyalty to Leonard Weste. That kind of loyalty is considered admirable among my own people. I might be able to convince them to spare you, if you would swear your allegiance and agree to fight for our cause. Of course, you would be required to adopt our ways and customs."

"What do you mean?" Santoso interjected. "Become a member of the JI? No, thanks—I'm no terrorist."

"We are not terrorists. We are freedom fighters."

"You can pour all the honey you like on it to make things taste sweeter, but the fact remains your cause is doomed to fail. So is this ridiculous get-rich-quick scheme Weste and Tan have cooked up. Believe me, when the shit hits the fan I plan to be as far away from here as possible."

"If you choose not to accept my offer now, there will not be a second chance," Hamzah replied. "I cannot guarantee protection from my people."

"No offense, but I don't need protection," Santoso replied. "Like I said, thanks, but no thanks."

17

"He went where?" Mack Bolan demanded.

Barbara Price cleared her throat, and said, "I don't know what's going on exactly. Hal wouldn't give me any more details than that. With you out of the country and the President scrutinizing our every move, I think maybe he felt useless and just wanted to get away. You know, do something to help out."

"Getting himself killed won't help out," Bolan said. "There's no doubt Tan's behind most of this. I don't know why yet."

"It does seem there are much easier ways to make money on the side as a DEA agent than what he's been doing all of these years," Price agreed. "We've got all the information you uploaded to our servers from the laptop, and Bear's working on it now. I'm sure we'll extract some type of pattern. What's next on your agenda?"

"I have a theory Tan's going to try leaving the country. If I can stop him before he does, we stand a pretty good chance of heading this off while there's time. What about the recall?"

"I'm not sure we can make it happen soon enough."

"Give me the problems."

"Well, the main one is logistics. More than half of all agencies west of the Continental Divide have already converged on L.A. We also know of commitments from DEA offices in Cheyenne, Denver, Santa Fe, Lincoln and Austin. So far, Hal's been incommunicado, which has left me to contend with everything imaginable here. I can't get the Man to call it off.

He says he doesn't want to interfere with agency response procedures. And Hal absolutely forbid me to make further contact with the Oval Office without his approval. I also got wind from a friend in the NSA that Homeland Security and BATF are now involved, as well."

Price's words demonstrated the gravity of the situation. Someone on high had pulled the panic switch, and Bolan couldn't be sure who or why. Without that information, he stood little chance of stopping it. This was a matter of pure bureaucracy. Of course, he'd suspected it would be difficult to keep the whole thing quiet when he'd first asked Amherst to keep his involvement low profile. That left Los Angeles and the surrounding towns open to street-level warfare if he didn't stop this thing and fast.

"Okay, I understand now," Bolan said. "Keep trying to contact Hal and if you reach him, let him know what we've discovered. Ask him to sit tight and don't do anything rash until I get back."

"I will, I promise. What are you going to do?"

"I need a couple more hours to wrap up things here," Bolan said. "As soon as that's done, we'll head back. Do what you can on that end to get us clearance out of here without delays. Jack's already getting the plane in shape for the return trip."

"Understood. Good luck," she told him. "And be careful there. I think we're going to need you for this one like possibly we've never quite needed you before."

"Never a dull moment," he quipped. "Out here."

Bolan disengaged the satellite phone and removed the earpiece. He steered the bullet-riddled sedan toward the same docks where he'd first encountered the *pechin.* Mercifully, night had fallen and the scarred body of the sedan wouldn't likely draw the attention of Jakarta police. The last thing the warrior needed was an encounter with local law enforcement. Bolan had always maintained a silent alliance with police officers, regardless of what country he encountered them.

He'd never dropped the hammer on a cop and wasn't about to start now. Bolan knew when he started to kill indiscriminately—never giving so much as a thought to those he viewed as brothers on the same side—that would be the day to call it quits.

Bolan and Grimaldi had disseminated enough of the information on the laptop to determine a boat was preparing to leave that particular port that night, and Bolan suspected it would have a massive quantity of drugs aboard. The Executioner planned to ensure that boat never left the docks, and he intended to also make certain Tan fell that same night.

It took him fifteen minutes to complete his journey.

Bolan parked the sedan a block away and went EVA. The MP-5K A-5 hung beneath his left armpit, the 96 Brigadier riding his right hip and he held the HK-53 in the ready position. Bolan had stowed the SPAS-12 shotgun in a makeshift holster constructed from webbing strapped across his back. Shells rode loosely in the concealed, easy-access slit pockets of his blacksuit and spare magazines for the HK-53 and MP-5K A-5 were taped together mirror-style and tucked into hip pockets.

Bolan reached the wharf and studied his surroundings. A muggy mist had settled on the docks, obscuring the moonlight. The warrior whispered silent thanks for the natural concealment and swiftly approached the building in a crouch. The neoprene soles of his boots didn't make a sound as he crossed to the exterior and pressed his back to the wall. He kept as low as possible, blending with the gloom and prepped for enemy contact. He'd decided on making a soft approach, but there wouldn't be anything quiet about what happened after that.

Bolan skirted the building, crossed to the dock and peered around the corner to find a dozen hands busily at work, pushing dollied crates up the gangplank of a midsize freighter. The warrior quickly assessed the immediate geography, mapped the best points of cover and concealment and sized up the approximate numbers of his enemy.

And then the Executioner stepped from the shadows and opened the ceremonies on his sworn enemy.

Bolan's assault against the *pechin* took them by total surprise. His first volley of 9 mm Parabellum rounds ripped away the jaw and arm of a guard who leaned against a railing on the freighter right at the point where it met the gangplank. The reports from Bolan's HK-53 drowned the man's shouts of pain as he dropped hard to the deck.

Two sentries near the entrance to the building swung their weapons to bear as they rushed Bolan's position. The Executioner went prone and fired at them. The first man caught a short burst to the gut, the rounds penetrating flesh and exposing entrails. The man slid face-first on the macadam and died. The second armed *pechin* realized the rashness of their tactic and tried to overcorrect by redirecting to cover. He never made it. Bolan triggered his weapon and delivered a salvo of rounds that nearly cut the guy in two.

Complete pandemonium erupted among the hired hands loading the ship; it appeared not all of them were Tan's religious fighters. It never ceased to amaze the Executioner how weak the staying power of some religious convictions when the bullets started to fly. Whoever said there were no atheists in a foxhole hadn't apparently included religious extremists in the count. Bolan watched a moment with amused satisfaction as the unarmed workers scampered down the gangplank or slid along mooring ropes to escape getting shot or otherwise maimed in the melee.

Just like rats abandoning the sinking ship.

Bolan regained his feet and rushed the two men he'd shot, searching for additional ammunition. Neither of their weapons was compatible with his 9 mm arsenal, but he did procure several Soviet-made RGD-5 hand grenades—they would prove handy ordnance in sabotaging the freighter so it couldn't leave.

While Bolan would have preferred to locate and execute

Tan, he realized disabling the freighter took priority. Bolan pocketed the grenades and charged up the gangplank, unimpeded by the workers, who were careful to give him a wide berth. Autofire greeted Bolan when he reached the top. The warrior shoulder-rolled to the cover of a large steam vent protruding from the deck of the ship. Bullets chewed into the deck plating and ricocheted off the polished iron of surface-mounted fixtures. Bolan waited for a lull in the firing before rushing to a new position that would offer him a better view of his assailants.

The Executioner risked peering around a corner but saw nothing. A fresh horde of rounds buzzed past his head and caused him to duck behind cover once more. When the firing stopped again, Bolan did a second check from another angle; this time lady luck smiled at him. The reflection of dock lights on metal revealed the position of his enemy on the observation deck ten feet above and straight ahead. Bolan raised his weapon before his opponents could target him and squeezed the trigger, this time for a sustained salvo. Screams rewarded his efforts as the rounds connected with a trio waiting on the observation deck. Bolan confirmed two died instantly. He ceased firing, convinced the third had suffered only a wound and crawled out of sight. In either case, he didn't pose a threat at the moment, and Bolan rushed to the base of the observation deck. Hitting him from directly above would be virtually impossible under that light and at those angles.

Bolan kept his back pressed to the wall as he sidestepped quietly and followed the angles of the deck base. He soon reached a door and quickly tried the handle. It gave freely and Bolan swung the door inward. He peered into the gloom and let his eyes rove up the steps that ascended to the observation deck. Slowly, Bolan made his way up the stairs, weapon held at the ready. The Executioner reached the top and poked his head through the top of the deck. He spotted the two bodies of his would-be attackers and then swept the area with the muzzle of his HK-53.

Only the faint sound of water lapping against the freighter greeted him.

Bolan waited another full minute before emerging onto the deck. He reached the steps of metal grating that rose to the bridge. There were no lights visible inside, and Bolan stopped to consider his options. If he destroyed the bridge using the grenades, it would likely be enough to disable the freighter and prevent its departure. However, he couldn't just assume Tan didn't have some type of backup plan; after all, he was dealing with the infamous Golden Dragon. Bolan mostly figured Tan would have a backup plan devised only to save his own neck. The drug product would be least of his concerns at this point.

Bolan considered those options, decided he didn't like the odds and continued past the bridge along the edge of the observation deck in the direction of the engine room. The only way to ensure the freighter didn't leave port would be to destroy the engines. If that took a few extra minutes, it was worth the price to make certain Tan couldn't complete at least part of whatever he had planned. The explosion would also be larger and more dramatic, and bring authorities running, doubly useful in making sure the freighter remained stationary.

It took Bolan only another six minutes to navigate the aft section and find his way to the engine room. The engines were already running, and the Executioner figured he didn't have much time before the freighter departed. What bothered him most was the minimal amount of resistance he'd encountered thus far. If Tan really wanted his plan to succeed, why wouldn't he have left a greater force behind to defend it? Surely he would have known Bolan had escaped by now.

Then again, Bolan could believe Tan's cocky attitude would have made him overconfident. The Executioner had learned overconfidence in oneself led to underestimation of the enemy. Still, Bolan had stormed this boat with no idea of the numbers he might face, and it had turned out to be a rather paltry force. So far, he'd encountered six armed *pechin,* of which five were confirmed kills and one—if not fatally wounded—injured to the point of impotency.

The Executioner checked his watch and noted it was close to midnight. Bolan quickly moved through the engine room, looking for any operators or mechanics on duty, but he didn't find anybody. So the engines were warming for an unknown departure, and only a skeleton crew was aboard with a minimal number of guards. A few seconds elapsed and then one word entered Bolan's conscious.

Trap!

The Executioner wheeled and headed for the engine-room exit. He sprinted along its length and when he reached the steps leading from the bowels of the ship, he vaulted them three at a time. Bolan steadied his breathing, pumping life-giving blood to his muscular legs as he continued up the steps. His calves threatened to cramp when he reached the top, but he lengthened his stride to keep them from failing him.

Bolan emerged from the boiler room and into the comparative coolness of the night air. He stopped to assess his options and instead of sprinting toward the stern of the ship and safety of the gangplank, he wheeled and headed aft as fast as he could. Bolan didn't stand on ceremony as he reached the stern. He dived over the railing, folding his body to ensure he cleared all moorings, and then snapped into a vertical position, feetfirst. He felt the rush of superheated air on his neck, heard the crackling of singed hairs as the freighter exploded. An orange glow emanated briefly around Bolan just before his body hit the water. It immediately cooled the superficial burns to his posterior as he submerged, dissipating all of the heat.

The Executioner continued down into the murky waters, keeping his eyes open despite the stinging saltwater. He used his powerful arms and legs to propel him through the water, moving away from the boat to avoid the risk of heavy debris dragging him to the bottom of a watery grave. Within two minutes his lungs burned, forcing him to surface.

Bolan's head bobbed on the waves in the aftermath of the explosion. Flames covered most of the boat deck, and Bolan could feel the heat from them even at his distance of about a hundred yards. He watched the freighter burn for another minute and then took another deep breath and submerged once more. Bolan eventually dragged himself from the water approximately three hundred yards from the freighter. He'd circle back to his vehicle and head straight to the airport.

With any luck, his clothes would dry out by then.

SONNY TAN LOWERED the binoculars with a smile. The flames from the freighter had the strangest effect on him, actually warming him from within. He turned and looked at Pane with unchecked approval.

"I cannot tell you how proud you've made me tonight, Jarot," Tan said. "Your idea to lure Cooper has succeeded. Now he's dead and we can proceed with our plans unhindered. I compliment you for your ingenuity. Now, go and see to it our plane is ready for departure. Our friends in the U.S. will be expecting us."

Pane bowed and left to do his master's bidding, but Tan could see the subtle hint of gloating in Pane's eyes. That was okay—he'd earned the right to gloat. With Cooper out of the way, nobody could know of their real plans. He considered the potential threat posed by Jack, but quickly dismissed his fear and doubt. What could one man do, and a pilot at that? In all likelihood, he was under instructions to pack it in and leave if Cooper didn't return after a certain amount of time. That would be just fine, because Tan had contacts everywhere and could arrange to make sure the pilot never left the country alive. After all, the Golden Dragon was capable of almost anything.

The murder of one lone pilot wouldn't prove to be any problem at all.

JACK GRIMALDI SAT in the spacious cabin of Stony Man's Gulfstream C-20 jet and double-checked his calculations for their return trip.

He stopped to check his watch. Bolan had indicated he would return within two hours, and only fifteen minutes remained. Grimaldi pushed the concern from his mind and worked to complete the computations necessary for the sophisticated onboard navigation computer. The plane had a maximum range of 3600 nautical miles. At a cruising altitude of 40,000 feet and speed of 441 knots, it would still take them more than fifteen hours to reach Los Angeles. Fortunately, the C-20 had in-flight refueling capability, which would reduce landing time significantly. It paid to work for a supersecret organization like Stony Man when the chips were down.

A scraping sound caught Grimaldi's ear, and he stopped penciling the figures into his worksheet. He cocked his head, hopeful Bolan had returned, but he didn't hear anything further. The plane had already been inspected, and Bolan wouldn't come through the airport with weapons. That, coupled with the influence Barbara Price had wielded on certain party members in government who owed certain favors, would expedite their departure on a considerable scale.

Grimaldi heard the scraping again. The pilot couldn't determine an exact source; it sounded like a damn cat shuffling across the wing. He flipped up one of the window visors and peered out. He detected no movement. Grimaldi shook his head and turned to his comp sheet once more. A third time had him out of the chair and headed to the door. He started to open it, then thought better of it. He went to the concealed weapons locker and removed his Colt .45. The pilot checked the action and load, then tucked it inside the elastic cuff of his flight suit and returned to the door. He slapped the release catch and the door slid upward obediently.

Grimaldi descended the steps with catlike movements. Years of training in savate hand-to-hand combat—along with his very slender form—had served the pilot well. While he wouldn't have touted his skills as equal to those of Bolan or the other Stony Man warriors, he could hold his own while doing plenty of damage in a scrape. Grimaldi reached the bottom step, and the noise he'd heard earlier became more pronounced.

This time, however, he heard it from directly behind him a moment too late.

A muscular forearm snaked around Grimaldi's neck and yanked hard, followed by a kick to the back of the right knee that took his balance. Muscles tensed in the arm of his unseen opponent and instantly cut off oxygen flow. Grimaldi tried to twist out and away by lowering his center of gravity, but the choker had too solid a position. The pilot forced himself to remain calm. Bolan had taught Grimaldi once that panic could be a warrior's fatal enemy. Right at that moment, he wished he had the Executioner there.

Grimaldi jumped straight up and tried to land on his assailant's instep, but the choker seemed to know that move, as well, and avoided the stomp. He slid a second arm under Grimaldi's left armpit and weaved it so his palm pressed against the back of the pilot's neck. The move exerted additional pressure, and Grimaldi felt a pulsing throb in his temples as his body tried to pump oxygenated blood to his brain. Stars danced in front of his eyes, and the pilot opened his mouth wide in an attempt to suck in enough air for one last attempt. The choker turned out to be too strong, as well as dwarfing Grimaldi in size, and as the pilot started to lose consciousness he wondered how he could have let something like this happen.

Grimaldi hadn't planned on dying like this.

Rims of blackness closed around the edge of his vision, and Grimaldi knew he had less than five seconds before the sleeper hold took complete effect. He could only feel his leg muscles now, every other nerve having obviously resolved to give up the fight already; his lungs burned and his heart pounded as if it would explode right from his chest.

And then it happened. He felt the sudden rush of air hit the back of his throat and reach his lungs in a microsecond. He could barely hear his own labored breath as he rasped and wheezed greedily for more. His mind still wanted to quit, but Grimaldi knew he couldn't let it happen. The pressure on his neck had significantly abated although the pain continued.

Grimaldi shook his head to clear the cobwebs and realized he'd landed on his knees. The pilot could hear a grunt behind him and turned, grabbing the back of his head to steady a painful complaint from his neck muscles, and saw the specterlike form of Mack Bolan. Grimaldi had to blink his eyes several times to be sure he hadn't imagined all of it—that he wasn't actually dying and saw visions of his life passing by—but the reality of it took over quickly enough.

Bolan stood in a ready stance, faced off against a man who had to be a third again his size. The Executioner stepped inward and launched a vicious side kick to the behemoth's knee. Grimaldi heard the crunch of the knee as it popped out of place even over the hammering in his ears. Bolan stepped closer and drove an elbow upward to catch his opponent on the chin as the man bent to grasp his displaced patella. The guy's head snapped back, blood and shards of teeth erupting from his mouth. Bolan continued the attack with unrelenting force. He fired a rock-hard punch to his opponent's midsection at the level of the diaphragm, then yanked the man forward and smashed a knee into his enemy's forehead. The giant's body went slack and he fell prone to the hangar pavement.

Bolan turned and rushed to Grimaldi. He extended a hand and pulled the pilot to his feet. Grimaldi stood there a moment on unsteady knees, his body shaking in the aftermath of oxygen-starved muscles fed by adrenaline. He couldn't remember the last time he'd come so close to meeting his Maker. Grimaldi could barely speak so he just rubbed his throat.

The Executioner, his friend and saving grace, clamped a firm but gentle hand on his shoulder. "You okay?"

The pilot nodded and asked hoarsely, "What kept you?"

"Time-bomb clearance sale downtown," Bolan replied with a smile.

"Tan?"

Bolan shook his head. "Gone, but I think I know where. And we have the added advantage because he probably figures both of us for dead. You still up to flying?"

"I'll get us up," Grimaldi croaked. He cleared his throat, grimaced at the pain and added, "Autopilot can take it from there."

"Come on," Bolan said, "let's get that throat on ice."

"Sounds to me like we could call your visit a success," Amherst told Brognola when he returned to the base of operations they had set up in the suite of a midpriced Hollywood hotel. In this case midpriced turned out to be about three hundred dollars a night. Brognola wouldn't have ordinarily bit quite so deeply into Stony Man's budget for mere extravagance, but this had become a priority and West Hollywood turned out to be the best location for a centralized operations structure.

"I guess it's all in how you look at it," Brognola replied. "Though I think I shook him up a bit."

"What did you have in mind for our next move?" Lareza asked.

"I don't want us to get in over our heads," Brognola said. "I want you two to get back to Weste's and set up surveillance. Take Amherst's SUV—it'll be much less conspicuous out there. Watch for anything strange, but mostly you should keep your eyes open for Santoso or Hamzah."

"I thought you said it wasn't likely they would go back there," Amherst said. "Seems to me a stakeout's just a time waster."

"Maybe, but I can't take chances," Brognola said. "While you're doing that, I'm going to recruit some help."

Without another word, the pair collected their gear and left. After they were gone, Brognola called Price at Stony Man Farm. He ran down the events of the past twelve hours, and described some of the different scenarios he'd formed about how Weste and his crew might be involved in the drugs. Price listened patiently to everything he had to say and then told him about the President, Sonny Tan and the status of Bolan's mission.

"So Kissinger's connection didn't turn out to be so good," Brognola said.

"That's only the half of it," Price replied. "Striker thinks he's working with terrorists on this drug deal. He just doesn't know why yet."

"That would fit into my theories about Hamzah. This thing has had the JI written all over it from the get-go." Brognola paused and considered their options. "How long before Striker can get here?"

"We've arranged for a USAF tanker from the 157th out of Pearl to perform an in-flight refueling. But even at top cruising speed, Jack estimated a good fifteen-hour flight time."

Brognola glanced at the clock radio on the bedside table and puffed air through his cheeks. "It's almost 1600hrs here now. That means touchdown at maybe 0800hrs tomorrow."

"Assuming they don't hit trouble and have to put down, that's about right."

"I'm not sure we can stall them that long. Did Striker have any ideas what Tan and the JI might actually have planned?" Brognola asked.

"It's looking more and more like the drugs are, and have been, of secondary consideration. Despite your cautions, I tried appealing to the Man one more time to let us work this thing further before allowing federal agencies to commit the manpower. He refused."

Brognola snorted. "I'm not surprised. Someone has really put a bug in his ear where it concerns us. And I'm not friendly to the notion you went against my express orders, Barb."

"I had to try," Price countered. "And you know it. Besides, it couldn't hurt to make the effort. Sometimes these things require a woman's touch."

That caused the Stony Man chief to laugh. He appreciated her sense of humor.

"Okay, so what are our options?" Brognola mused aloud. "Striker will get here as soon as he can. Is Able Team back yet?"

"No, they're still tied up in Miami."

"I don't want to have to call Phoenix Force in on this, but I may not have a choice. Sitting on my hands won't make things better."

"You may have the time," Price said. "I understand from my sources at the NSA that full mobilization and deployment to L.A. won't be finished until day after tomorrow. That's going to give you plenty of time to lay low and wait for Striker's backing."

"It still seems like a bad way to go," Brognola said. "I've deputized Amherst and this Sergeant Lareza as U.S. marshals. That should keep me fortified until Striker gets here, like you say. Did you come up with anything more on our friends this morning?"

"Their identities are still being sorted out, but it looks like they may be members of the JI. At least one of them has been identified as having political ties with Indonesian radicals."

"All right," Brognola said. "Keep me apprised. And Barb?"

"Yes."

Brognola cleared his throat before he said, "Thanks for trying."

"You bet. Be safe, Hal."

"See you," he replied, and disconnected the call.

While he wouldn't have admitted it openly, it did the Stony Man chief good to hear Bolan was on his way back. He'd longed to have the Executioner's expertise and counsel in this whole god-awful mess. It had been quite some time since he'd last been in the field on an active mission. And the years—while they hadn't been necessarily unkind—hadn't exactly been carefree and unstressed.

Brognola turned to the documentation spread before him on his bed. He studied the paperwork a moment longer, and then kicked off his shoes and propped himself against the headboard with pillows. No point in being uncomfortable while he worked. Brognola picked up the near ream of paper and began to sort through the dossiers he had on Santoso, Hamzah and Weste. He wasn't sure what he sought, but he considered the possibility something might jump out at him with time and effort.

Nearly two hours elapsed before he finally put down the paper. His stomach growled with the gnawing pangs of hunger, and acid began to rise in his throat.

Brognola reached into his pocket and withdrew the antacids he consumed like candy, then looked at the clock and realized he'd spent enough time scrutinizing the intelligence. This wouldn't help him any.

Brognola reached down to toss the documents aside when something interesting caught his eye about halfway down the fifth page of Leonard Weste's file. It seemed the movie mogul had a number of real-estate holdings not located in the greater Los Angeles area. In fact, he had estates all over the country, but the one thing that piqued Brognola's interest had to do with an abandoned movie lot located just off State Road 86, out near Salton Lake.

Brognola reached to the phone and called Stony Man. "Bear, I need you to give me some information on the following number." The big fed gave him the telephone number listed for the studio and had him check phone records to see if it was still active.

"Affirmative," Kurtzman replied. "What's the deal, Hal?"

"I'm not sure, but it could be the best lead I've had on this thing," Brognola said. "Can you pull up Weste's phone records and see if he's made any calls to the place recently?"

Brognola could hear rapid-fire clacking as the fingers of Stony Man's resident computer expert danced across the keyboard. He waited with bated breath, the excitement building in his mind. The place would probably provide a perfect location for Hamzah or Santoso to keep their heads down. It could also work out to be Brognola's trump card, and allow the Stony Man chief to crack the plot wide-open.

"Well?" he prodded impatiently.

"It's coming up now," Kurtzman replied easily. "Yeah, yeah...there were three calls made to that place this morning from Weste's residence phone. Hold on, I'll check to see if there are any from his cellular phone."

"No time," Brognola said, leaping from the bed. He asked if Price was immediately accessible.

"Negative," he said. "She went to the farmhouse to catch a few winks."

"Okay, let her sleep," Brognola said. He gave Kurtzman the address. "Tell her I went there to see if I can find Hamzah and Santoso. If I don't report back within six hours, send the locals to find me and get Phoenix Force on a plane."

"Roger that," Kurtzman said. "Watch your ass out there, Hal."

Brognola grunted in way of reply and hung up the phone. He slipped into his shoes, donned his jacket and left the room. Two minutes to ride the elevator to the parking garage and another four to wait for the valet to get his car, put him on the road in under ten minutes. He estimated the drive at shy of two hours. It wouldn't be crowded this time of year, since tourist season didn't begin for a few months yet.

Brognola increased speed once on the highway, headed for a possible appointment with the architects of terror.

BART WIKERT STARED with smug satisfaction at the room full of federal agents. The boys from the FBI were here in force, sure, but also they had agents from Homeland Security detachment—just like he and Howard Starkey—who belonged to DEA, BATF, and there were even some guys from the NSA. Every federal law-enforcement agency was represented in that room, and rumor control had it more guys were on their way. It looked like their play with that dumb-ass judge had paid off after all.

"Okay, okay," Wikert said, waving his arms. "Let's everybody quiet down and grab a seat."

The men filed to whatever available seats they could find, and the roar of conversation quieted to more of a rumbling din. Wikert knew that he and Starkey could count themselves a fortunate pair. This had been their baby from the very beginning when the drugs started funneling into Los Angeles and other major Western cities like a narcotics free-for-all. It didn't make a good goddamn what that sanctimonious asshole from the Justice Department thought. This multijurisdictional task force—one of the largest ever assembled for an operation of this kind—now waited to implement Wikert's brainchild.

Wikert and Starkey had watched the drugs pile up in L.A. for months now. It had slipped by customs through every mode of transportation imaginable. Wikert and Starkey simply sat back and continued to collect the intelligence, waiting for the day they would have enough evidence to put it all together and get the warrants needed for the task force. They had code-named the operation Dead Horse, and they were now less than twenty-four hours from the largest simultaneous execution of search-and-seizure warrants ever attempted in the entire world.

"Okay, stow it!" Howard Starkey demanded. The last of the talking died down and Starkey turned the floor over to Wikert.

"Welcome, men," Wikert said. "Welcome to Operation Dead Horse. I'm SAIC Bart Wikert. My partner here is Howard Starkey. I hope you signed on for some action, because you're sure as hell going to get it. I'll give you just a little background as I know most of you have already been briefed in detail by your commanding officers. In short, members of one of the largest heroin and opium cartels in the eastern world have brought nothing less than a drug circus to this country. Their distribution system has focused the pipeline efforts on two major areas, Los Angeles and Seattle.

"Up until now, the FBI offices up there that were originally established to work with Seattle on their increased gang activity have been able to handle things quite effectively without the assistance of outside agencies. Under normal circumstances, something like this would be headed up by the DEA, but these are not normal circumstances, unfortunately. Are there any questions so far?"

One agent standing in back raised his hand and was recognized. "Reports I've seen say we may be dealing with several major gangs here, sir. Could you confirm or deny that intelligence with certainty?"

Wikert nodded. "Absolutely I can, and I believe it's quite true. Just recently my partner and I witnessed a major shoot-out between rival gangs. In fact, we witnessed more than one. We attribute the increased violence to the influx of drugs—hence the reason we have multiple agencies like the BATF and ourselves involved."

"Thank you, sir."

"So, back to the plan," Wikert said. He turned and withdrew a laser pointer from the breast pocket of his coat. He began pointing it at a map of the greater L.A. area and indicated areas shaded in red, green and blue. "At exactly noon tomorrow, gentlemen, we're going to execute perhaps one of the largest coordinated police efforts ever undertaken. At a predetermined signal, our teams split into three jurisdictions, as indicated here, here and here, will serve warrants against those places warehousing unprocessed heroin and opium. Be assured, our intelligence is very reliable on all of these areas. It's highly unlikely any of our teams won't find drugs, and you will most likely take the occupants of the warehousing operations by total surprise.

"The stepped-on value of these drugs is currently estimated at close to one billion dollars. This will not only be one of the largest coordinated raids ever conducted, but it will also be the single greatest drug seizure in terms of monetary value ever conducted. Your team leaders will have the details of your assignment and orders. I would suggest all of you get a good night's sleep, gentlemen, because tomorrow you're going to make history."

Wikert dismissed them without much ceremony, then headed back to the FBI-rented apartment he shared with Starkey.

The Stony Man chief parked his car a couple blocks away from the abandoned movie lot and navigated the open field on the back side of the property line. As he got within range of the fence bordering the lot—its condition hadn't held back trespassers for years—movement caught Brognola's eye. He crouched and continued to the fence line, then brought a pair of miniature binoculars to his eyes. Brognola adjusted the focus and studied the lone building that remained standing.

Oddly, a light emanated from the edges of one of the many plywood sheets used to board up the place. Like the fence, it had suffered some significant abuse, but still clearly faired better than the buildings surrounding it. Brognola watched the building with anticipation, looking for the source of the movement, but he couldn't see much. The binoculars he'd picked up at a Thrifty-Box Mart near the hotel were neither powerful nor equipped with night-vision technology. They obviously would have been more appropriate for observing sporting events from the cheap seats than sensitive operations.

Brognola lowered the binoculars and considered his options. Crossing that open ground on foot would be suicide if hostiles occupied the house. He considered contacting local police for backup, but that would take too long, and he might miss the opportunity to capture Santoso and Hamzah. Calling Amherst and Lareza for assistance would also waste a lot of time. No, if he stood any chance of closing in on his quarry at all, he'd have to act now.

What was it the men of Able Team were always saying? Just nut up and do it!

Brognola grinned at the thought as he returned to his car. He dropped the binoculars through the open driver-side window and then popped the trunk. He reached inside and withdrew a Remington 870 tactical shotgun. A recent addition to the Remington line, the model Brognola had selected featured an 18-inch barrel with a 2-shot magazine extension, adjustable length-of-pull stock and a spring-loaded cam to absorb recoil.

Brognola checked the action, pumped a shell into the breech and then carried the weapon to the front with him and climbed behind the wheel. It had been just a few years ago when a certain large, icy-eyed soldier had lectured Brognola at length about his being too valuable to ever conduct field operations again. While the Stony Man chief treasured his friend's advice, he also realized that sometimes a leader had to demonstrate he could kick a little ass when times called for it.

To Brognola's way of thinking, this was one of those times.

Brognola started the sedan's engine, whipped the vehicle around and jumped the curb. He rode the slight incline beyond the curb until reaching the comparatively level ground of the field, then picked up speed. The sedan bounced and jounced along the uneven terrain of dried grass mixed with rocks and sand—the shocks and struts chirping in protest with the nastier points—and it took all of Brognola's focus to keep from damaging the vehicle before he reached his mark. Having to keep his lights off didn't help much, either.

At one point, Brognola left his seat and hit his head on the roof. He rubbed it absently as he continued to increase speed. A couple dozen yards before the fence line the ground flattened. Brognola had done his best to estimate where the chain link would be weakest and not prove too much trouble for the sedan. He guessed right as the vehicle plowed through the fence, tearing that section away from the top and driving right over it.

The wheels hit rough pavement, and Brognola had to compensate to keep from fishtailing. He quickly regained control and headed for the house. He couldn't be absolutely sure this had been his brightest moment, but something in his gut—that intuition he'd learned to heed over the years—told him something stunk to high heaven about the occupants in the abandoned house on this lot. He couldn't buy indigents or homeless. No, coincidence didn't exist in Brognola's book.

The Stony Man chief had less than fifty yards to go before he encountered trouble. He spotted a flash in his peripheral vision and turned in time to see something rocket toward him, leading just enough so that it would make contact perfectly. Brognola grabbed the shotgun, whipped open the door and bailed in the nick of time. The grenade contacted his sedan a moment later, and the car erupted into a fireball with enough heat to singe Brognola's eyebrows.

The big fed looked for cover and found a large, broken chunk of concrete ten feet to his right. He rolled to cover and brought the shotgun out in front of him. The Stony Man chief held his position, waiting for a second rocket to end it, but it never came. Brognola watched helplessly as his vehicle, now a veritable flaming missile, continued onward and plowed into the back of the house. Secondary explosions ensued as the tires popped under the heat and the gas fumes caught.

Brognola watched the area ahead, looking for either the grenadier or other enemy targets. A moment later two shadowy figures loomed into view, partially illuminated by the crackling flames. Brognola kept as low as possible, convinced by the pair's behavior they hadn't seen him yet. They approached with caution, keeping low while they moved in leapfrog fashion. Brognola remained as still as a corpse until they were practically on top of him, and then he let loose with the shotgun.

The first guy he took at nearly point-blank range. The 12-gauge No. 2 steel double-aught shot eviscerated the guy. The enemy gunner was nearly cut in two. The man screamed and dropped his Uzi SMG as the force blew him backward and dumped him on his back. Brognola rolled as he pumped in a new shell, got to one knee and blew away the second target with a full burst to the chest. Pink, frothy sputum erupted from the man's mouth. His body twitched like a string puppet, and Brognola could see a puff of lung tissue and blood with every wheeze. The man finally dropped to his knees and fell forward onto his face, dead before he hit the ground.

Autofire punctuated the night air. Rounds buzzed past Brognola's head like a swarm of disturbed hornets. The big fed turned to see what amounted to a small army round a front corner of the house and head straight for him. Brognola worked the pump of the shotgun, extended his arm and fired a shot to keep heads down while he rushed for the dropped Uzi.

Even from a distance, Brognola could tell the men were dark-skinned. They weren't wearing any distinguishing clothing, but he didn't have to guess he was facing JI terrorists. There couldn't be any other possible explanation. Brognola reached down, scooped the Uzi from the dust and triggered the weapon. Flame spit from the muzzle as Brognola sprayed the enemy position with 9 mm Parabellum rounds. The terrorists fell under the assault, some screaming, some silent, while others—obviously a bit disoriented by Brognola's vicious offense—searched frantically for cover. Even at those moments he scored confirmed hits, Brognola knew his luck wouldn't last long in this situation. The terrorists had him outmanned and outgunned, and the Reaper would only be patient so long. He had to get the hell away from this stingers' nest while still in one piece.

Brognola took his eyes from the carnage long enough to locate the other weapon. He backed up to the position, delivering a fresh volley to keep heads down and secured the SMG.

He couldn't immediately identify it, but he guessed a Czech-made Model 61 Skorpion; he hadn't seen one in some time. Brognola spotted another broken hunk of building, this one a bit larger, and rushed toward it. With luck, he could hold off the enemy long enough to either escape or bring the cops calling.

And right then he cursed himself for not having heeded Mack Bolan's advice.

BART WIKERT STIRRED as the sun peered over the horizon, the red, orange and purple cloud cover signaling dawn's awakening.

Wikert climbed from bed and headed straight for the bathroom. He showered, dressed and headed for the coffeepot he'd set to brew automatically. He retrieved the newspaper left at the door of their hotel and read it over coffee and cigarettes while Howard Starkey rose and went through his own morning routine. When both men were ready, they drove straight to a meeting room they had commandeered at the L.A. Federal Building, and began to issue last-minute instructions to the men who filtered in.

Wikert had spent hours ensuring this thing went off without a hitch. Sector Green would be to the south around Carson and Lakewood, led by Starkey. Sector Red, which Wikert had chosen to supervise, would handle all the strike areas in Inglewood. John Rowland, another FBI agent from the Reno office, would handle Culver City and West Hollywood to the north, aka Sector Blue. After a final briefing and equipment check, the men split into their teams and headed for their areas of operation.

The time had come for Operation Dead Horse.

AS SOON AS THEIR PLANE WAS in the hangar, Bolan and Grimaldi headed straight for the hotel in West Hollywood where Brognola had set up shop. During their drive to the hotel,

Bolan contacted Stony Man and got an update: the situation wasn't good. Nobody had heard from Brognola since his call to Kurtzman the night before.

"The last of Phoenix Force arrived just a while ago," Barbara Price advised. "I was about to dispatch them to your location."

"Hold off," Bolan said. "I don't think it's wise to bring them in on this quite yet. Just tell David I think it's better they remain on standby until I can get my teeth into this. He'll understand that."

"But we're talking about Hal, Striker," Price said.

"Yes, we are. And I don't want to muddy the waters by increasing the number of combatants on this thing."

Price couldn't argue with his logic, even unspoken, and they both knew it. Los Angeles had already reached the verge of becoming a war zone, and in an operation that large being certain of your enemy could get damn fuzzy. Bolan would be walking a fine line as it was, and to involve highly specialized commandos using military tactics—even for a discriminating and disciplined team like Phoenix Force—could buy everyone more trouble than they needed.

"Can you at least tell me what you're planning to do?" Price said. "I'm not going to be able to keep Hal's name out of this with the Man much longer. He knows something's about to go down soon, and if the going gets tough he'll expect answers."

"I understand," Bolan said. "Just minimize contact like Hal said. I think I know what Tan and the JI might be up to, and I have a plan. I'll be in touch."

Bolan broke the connection and filled Grimaldi in on the details. Then he said, "I've been thinking a lot about Tan."

"Oh, yeah?"

Bolan grunted his assent. "Why all this building up his legend of the Golden Dragon and hiring religious fanatics just to secure a pipeline into the U.S.? And then when we call his bluff, he's willing to sacrifice it all to maintain a partnership with Hollywood bigwigs and Islamic terrorists. Then it fell into place. I think terrorist leaders in major drug-producing countries like Afghanistan and Myanmar saw an opportunity in Tan's little empire. I think they approached him with a plan to flood the U.S. market with drugs to draw massive federal agencies to the area."

"You're figuring the whole thing's staged so that once those agencies converge on Los Angeles, they'll commit a major strike against law enforcement? Sounds pretty elaborate, Sarge."

"No more elaborate than 9/11," Bolan countered. "Think about it, Jack. This could have gone down any number of ways and in any number of locations. Smuggling smaller caches through various ports is less risky and much more effective than dumping all your eggs in one basket. Why choose Los Angeles? Why push the entire drug product through one city and risk losing it?"

"Hasn't really seemed to be about drugs, has it?" Grimaldi admitted.

"No," Bolan replied. "I've worked every angle of this including gangs, politics and even organized crime. Any which way you spin it, it keeps coming back to the JI and religious extremists."

Grimaldi nodded. "It has all the earmarks for a major terrorist attack."

"Exactly," Bolan said.

"So what are we going to do?"

"You're going to take it easy," Bolan told his friend. "I think you've taken your fair share of a beating on this mission. From here forward, I'll work it alone."

They didn't speak for the rest of the trip to the hotel, each man lost deep in his own thoughts. The Executioner spent the silence formulating his plan. It seemed likely from all of Stony Man's intelligence that the multiagency task force would try for a coordinated strike. Since Bolan couldn't be in more than one place, he'd have to get the enemy to come to him. What he hadn't figured out yet was just how to do that. For now, he'd have to play it by ear and wait for an opportunity to present itself.

When they reached the hotel, Bolan used his DEA credentials to get them into the suite, assisted by a call-ahead from Stony Man Farm. Bolan sensed a presence as soon as he stepped through the doorway. He brought his Beretta 93-R into action and scanned the room. A door stood ajar on one side, and Bolan approached with Grimaldi covering him from the doorway. The door suddenly opened wide when Bolan got within a few feet of it, and a familiar face peered at him over the barrel of a semiautomatic pistol.

The pair relaxed simultaneously, and Captain Rhonda Amherst shook her head with a laugh. "I always wondered between us who was quicker on the draw."

Bolan nodded. "Where's Hal?"

"I don't know," Amherst said. "We just got back from the surveillance a few hours ago and he was gone. Looked to me like he left some time last night."

Bolan knew he'd heard the truth and holstered his Beretta. "It's likely he's in some serious trouble. I came into some info on his possible whereabouts. I'm going to check it out, but first I need your help."

"What can I do?"

Grimaldi had entered the suite and closed the door. The pilot headed straight to the refrigerator to get some ice for his throat. It had bothered him quite a bit throughout the trip, causing his neck to stiffen up a number of times. He couldn't find any ice in the compact refrigerator supplied with the suite, but one of the chilled bottles of Perrier would suffice as a makeshift cold pack. He immediately pulled it from the fridge, sat down on the sofa and propped his feet up while he applied the bottle to the right side of his neck.

"I think I've figured out what all of this is about," Bolan

said. He quickly briefed her on Sonny Tan, aka the Golden Dragon, and his possible affiliation with Weste.

"Well, that makes some sense now," she said.

"What's that?"

"Hal paid a visit to the LASD yesterday. Apparently, he spoke personally to Max Garner. The sheriff. *My* boss...or at least he used to be."

"Did he mention if he suspected Garner was in on it?" Bolan asked.

"I don't think he knew for sure," she said. "And he strikes me as too much of a professional to have mentioned it without incontrovertible proof."

"He's a professional leader, yes," Bolan replied, feeling a bit of angst that his friend would run off on some cowboy crusade. "But he's not a professional combatant. At least not anymore, and for all I know, he's already dead. What was it that made sense?"

"Huh?"

"When I mentioned Weste, you said something made sense."

"Well, I guess Brognola got Weste's name from Garner. He went to see him, basically to shake him up. The two guys you took out back at Montavo's yacht?"

Bolan nodded. "Yeah, I know. Santoso and Hamzah are working for Weste. One's connected to the Jakarta underworld and the other's a devout member of the JI. I think Tan's in bed with them, and that puts him in bed with Weste."

"Well, Brognola obviously thought so because he had us stake the place out," she said.

"See anything interesting?"

She nodded and led him over to the table. She retrieved a digital camera from it, flipped the power switch, then let her fingers dance over the various buttons and such until she found what she wanted. She passed the camera to Bolan for a look.

"That guy arrived early this morning at Weste's place," she said. "We managed to get a picture of him with the zoom lens on this camera Brognola supplied. The guy has some of the coolest gadgets."

Bolan recognized the features immediately. "Sonny Tan."

"That's your guy? Looks like you were right again, Cooper."

"Here's our problem," Bolan said as he passed the camera back to her. "We've identified all the players, but we still don't know the exact targets. It's my guess the task force they've been filling with agents from all over the country will attempt a coordinated strike against the drop points identified by your intelligence unit."

"Sounds about right."

"Outside of yourself, I don't know who else might know that," he continued. "You got any ideas where this task force might strike?"

"I don't, but I sure as hell know somebody who does."

"Max Garner," a voice from the other room said.

Bolan whirled and dug for his pistol, but Amherst stayed his hand. "Hold up, Cooper. He's on our side for sure."

Nesto Lareza walked across the room and extended his hand. As Bolan shook it, Amherst introduced them.

"I've heard a lot about you, Cooper," he said. "I saw your handiwork at Antoine Pratt's. Nice job."

"He needed a wakeup call," Bolan said.

He turned back to Rhonda. "What do you think about Garner?"

"I used to like him," Amherst admitted. "But after these past few months, seeing how he's ignored these problems and manipulated my best friend into thinking I'm in cahoots with drug dealers? Well, right about now I'd like to pop a cap in his ass."

Bolan grinned at that. "Maybe you'll get the chance. But

20

It didn't take the Executioner long to locate Sheriff Maxwell Garner.

Why, of course the sheriff knew all about the operations of the multijurisdictional task force. At least, that's what his personal assistant wanted Bolan to think. And could he be located quickly, because DEA Agent Matt Cooper needed to speak with him as quickly possible? So the pretty assistant with the long blond hair made a phone call to his personal line. Garner agreed to meet Bolan at a coffee shop near the sheriff's headquarters, but when Maxwell Garner parked his car, Bolan gained entry through the back door and hauled the sheriff back into his seat as he was exiting.

Bolan pressed the cold muzzle of his .44 Magnum Desert Eagle against the side of Garner's neck. Garner watched the man through his rearview mirror, and when he saw those ice-blue eyes and the grim visage staring back at him, he felt almost compelled to wet his pants. What he didn't know was he hadn't been the first man to feel like that after gazing into the death mask worn by the Executioner.

"I'm going to ask some questions, Garner," Bolan said. "You're going to answer them."

"S-sure, buddy," he said. He tried to smile and look relaxed. "Just watch what you're doing there with that gun. There's no need for violence, after all."

"Precisely what I'm trying to prevent," Bolan said. "First question, where is the task force planning to hit?"

"What task force?"

Bolan pressed the muzzle tighter against Garner's neck. "That's a question, not an answer. Try again."

"Okay, okay," Garner stammered. "There are three main locations, all centered around Inglewood."

"Who's in charge of it?"

"Guy named Wikert. Bart Wikert, I think."

Bolan felt the hairs stand on his neck. He knew Wikert's background quite well, along with that of his partner, Howard Starkey. He'd learned a lot about these two men, actually, after he'd caught them watching him and warned their superiors to shut down their surveillance. Bolan hadn't ever imagined they would be involved in this thing. Apparently, Wikert wielded a bit more influence than any of them realized. Bolan had made the critical mistake of underestimating a potential enemy who, in complete irony, he would now have to win over as an ally.

"Where do I find him?" Bolan asked.

"I can't remember," he said. "I have the address written down. It's in my shirt pocket."

"Get it carefully," Bolan said.

Bolan then instructed Garner to contact Weste and say Tan had stored all the drugs at his production warehouses just north of Studio City. Garner listened to Bolan's instructions intently and contacted Weste as soon as Bolan had left. He then began to craft the letter of resignation the stranger with the cold blue eyes had declared to be in the sheriff's best interest.

BART WIKERT PACKED his gear and took the federal-building elevator to the parking garage. He'd sent his team ahead with orders to deploy throughout Sector Red and await his arrival. Wikert reached his Chevy Suburban and loaded his gear into the backseat. He opened the front door to find Bolan sitting in the passenger seat.

"Cooper," Wikert said with a sneer. "What the hell are you—"

"Get in," Bolan replied. "We need to chat."

"Go to hell, Cooper. I got nothing to say to you. You don't have any juice with me, and I found out you no longer have any authority over me. I've been promoted to an SAIC, which if I'm not mistaken puts me well above *your* pay grade. So, yeah, I'm getting in but you're getting the hell out."

Bolan sighed and looked out the front windshield. He'd hoped they could do this amicably, but he also figured he stood a chance meeting this kind of resistance.

"Look, Wikert, I know I put a gun to your head on our first date, which probably didn't win me any brownie points."

"You're goddamn right!"

Bolan stared hard at the agent. "But if we don't put aside our differences here and now, you stand to lose a lot of good men. I'm trying to prevent that."

Wikert reached inside his jacket. "You know what, buddy, I've had enough of you."

"Don't," the Executioner warned. "Keep your hands where I can see them and I'll do the same. I want a five-minute white flag. If what I say doesn't change your mind, I'll bail and you won't hear from me again."

Wikert stared at Bolan a moment, but he'd stopped reaching for his weapon. Bolan kept his expression passive. He couldn't afford to agitate the guy at this critical juncture. Yeah, so Wikert had an ego but something told Bolan that deep down this guy genuinely cared about his country and his men. He'd learned to read for leadership qualities innate to individuals over the years, and Wikert struck him as a guy who would listen to reason if presented with a strong enough motivation.

Wikert shook his head, but took his hand from his coat and

jumped into the driver's seat. He closed the door and said, "Okay, you got five minutes. Talk."

"You and your task force are walking into a trap," Bolan said.

"Shit, I *knew* it! See, this is what I'm talking about. You've been trying to interfere with this operation from the beginning!"

"You promised me five minutes," Bolan said.

"Sorry," Wikert said. "I did. You claim we're walking into a trap. What sort of trap could someone set for more than fifty federal agents trained in special operations and armed to the teeth?"

"How about a large force of Jemaah Islamiyah terrorists? And bear in mind they have surprise on their side."

"Islamic fanatics? In Los Angeles?" Wikert screwed up his face. "Hard to believe."

"That's what they said about terrorists hijacking planes on U.S. soil and running them into heavily populated buildings," Bolan reminded him.

"All right, okay, so why would the JI be any threat to my task force?"

"They've always been the threat. This was never about drugs, but that's what we were meant to think. Slowly, probably over the past year or two, the JI has been smuggling its people into the country. They used the drugs as an excuse to flood the market until it got so bad, the U.S. government would have to act."

"So what?" Wikert said. "Major heroin imports haven't been a problem in this country for a real long time. Who needs it with all the crack, ecstasy and pharmaceutical combos these days?"

"That's exactly what makes the JI's plan so ingenious, Wikert. When drug product of that purity reaches a market potential so great it corrupts public officials, police and even members of the DEA, what do you think Uncle Sam's going to do?"

"Exactly what we are doing," Wikert said.

"Right, and that's what the JI's counting on."

"But how would they even know where we're going to strike?"

"Inside information."

"From who?"

Bolan let out a sigh. "That's the intelligence you haven't been given. I've spent the last seventy-two hours tracking this thing to its source in Indonesia. Over there, a DEA agent named Sonny Tan started his own cult of religious fanatics in a get-rich scheme. He probably would have succeeded, too, until his greed blinded him so much he climbed into bed with terrorists. Tan suffered from overconfidence, the same thing you're suffering from right now."

"Watch it, Cooper." Wikert jammed in a finger in Bolan's direction. "You still haven't convinced me. All I've got is a lot of hearsay."

Bolan waved away Wikert's show of indignation. "How do you think I know all of this? How do you think I knew where to find you? There are more fingers in this pie than you realize but if you don't squelch your ego, the blood will all wind up on your hands. You want that?"

Wikert stared at Bolan a moment and then shook his head. "No, not really."

"Good. Now, I have a plan to wrap this up nice and tidy, but I can't do it without your total commitment."

"I'm not turning this operation over to you, Cooper."

"I don't want it. This isn't about credit. You can have it. In fact, I'd prefer when this is over you keep me out of it entirely. Agreed?"

"Okay, I'm listening. But just tell me one thing first."

"What?"

"Why all your interest in this?"

"Outside of not wanting to see a bunch of good men get drawn like sheep to the slaughter? Despite what you think about me, I actually care what's going on. And these people may be responsible for the death of a very close friend, or at best his disappearance. That good enough for you?"

Wikert nodded. "Fair enough. What do you need from me?"

"Tan's main contact here in the States has been a Hollywood heavyweight named Leonard Weste. You heard the name?"

"From Weste-Tantamount Capital?" Wikert grinned. "Who the hell hasn't?"

Bolan nodded and continued, "Weste has two guys working under him, Maki Santoso and Shihab Hamzah. Santoso's a liaison between Weste and Tan. Hamzah's a member of the JI. I don't think Weste knows that, but it seems like we could make good use of that. What I want you to do is get the word out to your people the target has changed."

"And that is?"

"Weste's production warehouses just north of Studio City." Bolan reached into his pocket and withdrew a paper with the address.

Wikert looked at the paper awhile, studying it as if it were a foreign language, and then returned his gaze to Bolan. "So why there? And what am I supposed to do with all my men?"

"Not a thing," Bolan said. "Keep them right where they are. If I'm wrong about this, your people may have to go with the operation as planned. But at least you won't go in blind. I've arranged to draw the JI to that location. It's remote and hasn't been in use for some time. If the JI buys the story, it's them who'll be walking into a trap."

Wikert looked sideways at Bolan and smiled. "You going to take them down all by yourself?"

Bolan's expression was grim. "That's about it."

"And what about all the drugs?"

"I'm sure they're right where the LASD's intelligence has said they are," Bolan said. "Probably the same targets you plan to strike. The difference is you won't have terrorists with automatic weapons waiting to cut you down when you make entry."

"Okay, so we can go with our plan," Wikert said. "You just want me to buy you some time."

"Look at it like this," Bolan said. "You'll be buying *both* of us some time."

Wikert looked through the front windshield and didn't say anything for a long time. Bolan let him chew on it rather than prattle on and on. It wouldn't do any good. Wikert had enough smarts that he could make up his own mind if left alone. He'd either buy Bolan's story as truth simply because it was too wild to believe otherwise, or he'd completely dismiss it and make the mistake of trying to haul the Executioner to jail.

After a heavy silence, Wikert said, "All right, Cooper. You got a deal. But if you cross me, or you're wrong about this, I'm going to make it my personal mission in life to hunt you down and kill you myself."

"I won't cross you," the Executioner replied. "And if I'm wrong, I'll already be dead."

BOLAN SCANNED the production warehouses through the scope atop his SIG-Sauer SSG 3000 sniper rifle. The warrior felt the sweat trickle down his face, as well as his neck and the small of his back. Fortunately, the breathable material of his blacksuit kept him moderately cool. Four DM-51 grenades hung from his load-bearing harness. The Beretta 93-R and .44 Magnum Desert Eagle were in their respective places. He wore the FN FNC strapped to his back. Bolan lay concealed behind the rear dual tires of a panel truck parked directly across the street from the warehouse entrance.

When Bolan completed his sweep of the area, he tracked to Amherst's position on the west side of the fence encircling the expansive property. She sat stock-still—seeming for all intents as disciplined as any good soldier—cradling the M-4 carbine from the Gulfstream C-20's armory. Bolan studied her a moment longer and then redirected his sight picture to the other side of the fence line. He settled the crosshairs on the face of Lareza, who had staged in similar fashion, armed with the M-16 A-4/M-203.

Bolan wouldn't have ordinarily involved either of these officers, but the situation was about as desperate as it came. Since he didn't know what kind of numbers he'd face, the Executioner figured it only prudent to have someone provide a little backup and covering fire. But he'd left them with strict instructions that this was all they should do.

"Under no circumstances are you to directly engage hostiles," Bolan told them. "You stay on the perimeter and watch my six."

Both of them swore they would follow orders, but neither of them sounded very convincing in that promise. He could only hope for their own sakes they'd let him handle it.

The Executioner looked at his watch. If his plan worked at all, it wouldn't be long now. As if on cue, Bolan turned at the thunderous noises produced by a truck engine down the street on his right. He watched as it completed its turn and headed for his position. It was an unmarked panel truck not too dissimilar to the one sheltering him, but one-third again as large. Bolan turned to see if the approaching truck had caught the attention of the security officer seated inside a shack at the front gates. His gaze traveled between the truck and the guard. Because the guard was probably an innocent, Bolan had determined it would be necessary to wait until the terrorists got well inside the property line before launching any type of assault.

The truck loomed close and slowed, and now the guard was on his feet and headed out of the shack. Bolan kept still, certain the occupants of the truck cab wouldn't see him given their proximity to his position. The truck started to turn into the gate and came to a halt with the drawn-out screech of brakes. The guard approached the passenger door and engaged someone in conversation. Bolan squinted through the scope and settled it on the side mirror of the truck. A moment before the truck eased through the gate, Bolan caught the features of a man with dark skin and a beard. He had on a baseball cap with the brim worn low.

The Executioner smiled with satisfaction—it looked as if his plan had worked. Bolan waited until the truck turned to the left on the interior roadway that ran one way along the perimeter, and aimed at the front tire. He estimated the distance, windage and lead time required in under three seconds, took a deep breath, let out half of it and squeezed the trigger. The rifle produced a whip-crack report as the round exited at a muzzle velocity of 800 meters per second. The 7.62 mm NATO round accomplished the job its designers had in mind, providing a superior first-round hit probability. The slug ripped through the front tire, deflected and traveled upward until it lodged in the bottom of the engine block.

The driver jammed on the brakes and brought the truck to a thudding halt. He jumped from the cab, and through the scope Bolan spotted a Steyr TMP clutched in his hands. The soldier needed no other confirmation as to the identity of the arrivals—these were definitely the hostiles he'd waited for. Bolan ran back the bolt of the SSG 3000 and chambered a fresh round. He reacquired a sight picture as the driver pounded frantically on the truck to alert his comrades, and squeezed the trigger once more. Bolan watched as the man's head split like a grapefruit and splattered the truck with blood and brain matter.

The Executioner broke cover and headed straight toward the guard shack. The man stood just outside in complete awe, astounded by what had just transpired before his eyes. As Bolan got close, the guard turned and saw him approach with rifle in hand. The guard, an older guy just out trying to make an honest living, started to fumble for his revolver.

Bolan raised a cautionary hand. "Hold up, troop. I'm one of the good guys."

The guard stopped only a moment, then movement caught Bolan's eye, distracting both of them from the standoff. The passenger had exited the vehicle to release the back latch of the door. In fluid motions, Bolan worked the bolt, raised the rifle, aimed and fired. The NATO slug entered through the guy's spine and out his stomach. Blood splashed onto the back door and slammed the guy against it, but not before he'd managed to unlatch the door.

The door slid up and an army of Jemaah Islamiyah terrorists erupted from it like ants from a smoked hill.

Mack Bolan's first reaction was to grab the guard by the collar and shove him toward the shack with firm orders to keep his head down.

He then dumped the sniper rifle as he reached for the FNC and swung the muzzle down into play. He'd left the weapon primed and the safety off in case he needed it quickly. Bolan's foresight and experience served him well once more as he got the drop on the terrorists before they could even ascertain the location and strength of their enemy.

Bolan triggered the FNC, keeping it low and tight. The first 5.56 mm triburst caught one guy in the guts, and one of the rounds passed through to contact the man immediately behind him. Bolan dropped to one knee before buying any return troubles and triggered a sustained salvo. One man took a double-tap to the chest while the guy next to him caught a slug in the throat. The two terrorists staggered into each other in shock mixed with pain and collapsed to the pavement simultaneously.

The remaining twenty or so JI gunners finally seemed to collect their wits and split off in every direction in search of adequate cover. Only a few tried to foolishly use the truck, not realizing they were making it easy for Bolan by bunching up and becoming prime targets. Bolan took full advantage of the situation and demonstrated their fatal error in judgment. He charged their position, firing one-handed to keep them down while yanking a DM-51 from his LBE harness. The grenade came away—its pin and sleeve retained by the strap—and Bolan tossed it underhand toward the truck. He changed direction and circled the truck on the far side to keep out of the terrorists' fire zone.

The grenade did the rest of the work nicely. It clattered to the pavement, bounced beneath the truck and blew directly under the fuel tank. The concussion fractured the tank, followed by heat and flame to finish the job. Gasoline fumes ignited and shot flames from both sides of the truck as the heat popped tires and lifted the chassis a few inches off the ground. All four terrorists who'd sought cover behind the truck were instantly immolated by the superheated gases. Bolan heard the screams of agony from the pathetic, human torches and he tuned them out. It would be a small, but hollow victory if they had been responsible for the death of Hal Brognola.

Bolan checked for any further threats in the immediate area, then keyed the microphone that connected him to Amherst and Lareza.

"Sitrep," he demanded.

Lareza spoke first. "From my position I make six targets headed for the closest building."

Bolan keyed the microphone again. "Acknowledged. Amherst, what's happening on your end?"

"I saw two go between the two warehouses, and another few swung around on my side."

"Understood. Both of you hold position until you hear from me. I'm going to start on your end, Lareza, so clear your line of fire before engaging any targets and try not to shoot *me.*"

"Copy that," Lareza replied with a strong laugh.

Bolan didn't bother making a point of the fact he'd been serious in that last comment. Lareza had some firearms training and completed a tour as a Marine in the first Gulf War. He could hold his own. Amherst, however, posed another matter. While she seemed like a competent cop and commanding officer, she didn't have a lick of military training.

She had undergone a rigorous orientation in using the AR-15, very similar to the M-4 in many respects. Bolan felt she could also hang if the going got really tough.

Undaunted, the Executioner jogged for the production warehouse closest to Lareza. He nearly choked on the rancid odors of smoldering combustibles and burning bodies. It hadn't been the first time he'd walked through a bloody battlefield like this one, and it wouldn't be the last. Bolan dropped the nearly spent magazine from the FNC and loaded a fresh one as he got closer to the warehouse. He reached an exterior wall and peered through the small opening of a window where a corner piece of glass was broken out. He couldn't see much in the darkened interior outside of what the sunlight illuminated near the windows.

Bolan kept below the line of the windows as he rushed to the corner and peered around it. The terrorists were not in sight. He looked to his right and spotted Lareza motioning toward the massive dock doors at the far end of the building. Bolan tossed him the okay signal, then sprinted to the doors and found one had been pried aside to make it passable for a human body.

Bolan squeezed through the opening and entered the old warehouse. The musty smell of disuse and age assaulted his nostrils. He pushed the distracting odor from his mind and attuned every sense to his surroundings. If he didn't locate the terrorists and end this quickly, the mission stood a good chance of failure. He couldn't afford to let even one of them leave alive. Bolan slowed his breathing and called on every combat instinct. Confident yet cautious, he proceeded deeper into the shadows of the warehouse. He quickly crossed the main section to get out of the open and continued until he reached a wall that ran parallel with a long table.

Bolan kept to the wall and moved along it with care, each movement measured. He knew, as the terrorists did, that the slightest noise out of either side could spell the difference between life and death. Occasionally, he spotted bits of plaster or broken objects made from plastic and pottery. A few of the pieces looked like molds. In the half-light they were almost indistinguishable, but Bolan guessed this had probably once served as the model shop for movie productions, albeit he'd never professed to be an expert on such things. He continued along the wall, weapon in battery and ready.

The scrape of a foot, likely the product of walking on a floor littered with debris, resounded behind him. It hadn't been all that loud in reality, but to Bolan it had been as thunderous as the report from his Desert Eagle.

The Executioner whirled to deal with any threat.

RHONDA AMHERST COULD SIT still no longer.

She hadn't thought much of Cooper's plan to take down the terrorists single-handedly while she and Lareza sat on the sidelines, and she wasn't about to go on this way. She *had* to do something; she couldn't help herself.

Amherst double-checked the action of her rifle to make sure it wouldn't fail if at any given moment it came to using lethal force in self-defense, then struck out toward the production warehouses. She felt a mere pang of guilt for disobeying orders, but in the long and short of it she was a deputized, U.S. marshal, which meant she wasn't really in Cooper's chain of command. Without Brognola, that basically made her a free agent. Having justified her actions as the means to an end, Amherst moved toward the buildings with renewed purpose. She could take care of herself; she didn't need some big protector to come rescue her. After all, she'd commanded entire units in one of the busiest police jurisdictions in all of L.A. County; and if that didn't demonstrate her abilities then nothing would.

Amherst reached the warehouse unscathed, and crouched. She kept her back to the wall and looked in both directions, then rose and began searching for a way in. She soon found an entrance door, and the lock didn't prove to be any problem for the M-4 carbine. A single round did a number on the mechanism.

Amherst pulled open the door and moved inside, keeping low and covering all points with the muzzle of her assault rifle. The rise of dust from the floor in the wake of her movements tickled her nose. She wanted to sneeze but resisted the impulse, unsure if it would give away her position. Not that it mattered—the terrorists knew someone was gunning for them.

Amherst made contact with the first terrorist less than two minutes after entering the building. The man actually wasn't expecting a woman, and he hesitated to fire on her. It cost him his life. Amherst brought the M-4 to her shoulder as she'd been trained to do and held back the trigger. The weapon delivered a 3-round burst to the terrorist's chest and drove him against a large, circular support. The man's head cracked against the unyielding concrete post, and he slid to the ground, dead.

Amherst shuddered at the sight, realizing for just a moment that she'd just committed her first kill. It wasn't an empowering sensation—not even close. There was no adrenaline rush, no surge of power. Nothing except the urge to retch uncontrollably. It made her head spin and she averted her eyes; it was not time to get queasy. Queasy could kill her and she didn't have any desire to die in some abandoned warehouse at the hands of terrorists.

Amherst continued on her quest to find and destroy the enemies of justice.

THE JI GUNNER LOOKED surprised when the Executioner whirled on him, FNC up and ready. The expression changed to shock mixed with pain as Bolan triggered a short burst that caught the terrorist in the midsection. His eyes seemed to pop out of his head as if somehow the pressure from the bullets had traveled all the way from his guts to his eye sockets, although Bolan reasoned the dim surroundings had actually manufactured the illusion.

The echoes of autofire died in time for Bolan to detect movement in his peripheral vision. The Executioner turned to see two terrorists run past and grab cover in an aisle approximately twenty yards away. Bolan crouched, ran down options and then detached a DM-51. This time he left the outer sleeve in place. He let the grenade cook off two seconds, then lobbed it gently over the rows of tables in a high, easy arc. Three seconds elapsed before he heard it hit the ground, followed by two seconds of silence. The sounds of panic and scrambling were cut short by the generous results of high-explosive PETN and 2 mm steel balls.

Bolan rose before the dust had settled and continued moving. With the four he'd neutralized outside and three more just now, that brought the count to somewhere between ten and fifteen terrorists remaining, and at least three in this building. He knew it wouldn't take long for the guard to get on the horn and advise the local cops. Since it was Hollywood, they'd come quick and in force, to boot. That didn't leave Bolan much of a window, and he hadn't been kidding about staying out of the picture.

"Lareza to Cooper, do you copy?"

Bolan stopped, crouched and checked his flank before keying up his receiver. "Maintain radio silence."

"I can't raise Rhonda," he said.

Bolan felt his blood run cold and the hairs stand up on his neck. He looked above him and saw the reason for concern. Two of the terrorists had managed to gain access to the rafters far above, and they were now at a vantage point that afforded them a good view of the majority of the place, not to mention the ability of raining down a hailstorm of lead on the Executioner. They realized this at apparently the same time as Bolan, because they opened up with a pair of AK-47s immediately. The distinctive reports from their weapons sent

Bolan scrambling for cover. It came in the form of a heavy steel table along his row that he actually discovered by whacking his head against it. Bolan crawled beneath the comparative safety of the table and waited out the assault.

At a lull in the firing, Bolan broke cover and opened up with a furious but controlled pattern of sustained fire. A flurry of rounds punched holes through the terrorists balanced precariously in the rafters of the warehouse. Sparks flew as some of the rounds ricocheted off the steel girders. The impacts drove both of them off their makeshift perches and they struck the ground with the sickly noises generated when bones and flesh slammed into concrete at a high rate of speed.

Bolan could hear the shuffle of feet and the opening of a door somewhere near him. It took him a moment to locate a stream of sunlight that indicated the remaining terrorist was trying to escape.

He keyed up his radio. "Lareza, I've got one running and probably headed for you. Take him out."

"Roger."

Bolan raced for the door where the terrorist had exited, just in case Lareza required backup. As he reached the doorway, he heard the unquestionable finality of the M-16 A-: one shot, another...then silence. Bolan emerged through the doorway in time to see a cloud of dust rise where the terrorist had collapsed. And then another sound started to work on Bolan's ears: sirens.

The Executioner keyed his radio as he headed for the other building. "Nice shooting. Now stall the police as long as you can."

"What about Rhonda?"

"You worry about your brothers in blue. I'll worry about Amherst."

Bolan killed the radio set and within a moment he located a door standing wide-open. He peered inside and the sounds of autofire immediately greeted him. The reports were staggered, and it sounded clearly like a fairly heady battle. Bolan could almost differentiate each weapon being fired, and one sounded distinctly like an M-4.

The Executioner shook his head. Amherst apparently had trouble with authority. Under other circumstances, she would have made a hell of an addition to the Stony Man team. Right now, she was compromising the success of his mission. Bolan followed the sounds and quickly located the participants. Somehow, Amherst had managed to get caught between two terrorists down at ground level and two more in separate locations on a catwalk along a side wall.

It was time to even the odds. Neither of the men above had appeared to notice Bolan yet, and the pair at ground level were not in a strategic spot. Certain he didn't have enough rounds left in the FNC to make it count, Bolan withdrew the Desert Eagle, sighted down the slide at one of the terrorists and squeezed the trigger. A 300-grain boattail slug crossed the intervening forty yards in approximately one-hundredth of a second. It caught the terrorist in the side of the neck and nearly decapitated him as it blew a plum-sized hole out the other side, taking flesh, blood and spinal bone with it. The terrorist's head bobbed clumsily on his shoulders, and then he slumped to the catwalk. Bolan tracked on the second terrorist and fired again. This time the bullet struck the breastbone and cracked it in two. The slug drove the man's body backward and he flipped over the railing of the catwalk.

Bolan got in motion before that terrorist's body hit the ground. He reached Amherst and said, "Mind telling me what you're doing?"

"Same as you," she said with a grin. "Trying to save the world."

"Next time, leave it to the professionals."

"Oh," she snapped, "that really hurts."

"Not as much as a bullet or torture," Bolan said.

The shots being fired at them by the remaining pair of

terrorists were sporadic, delivered more in hope of a lucky shot than anything tactical.

"Once more, it looks kind of bad for the good guys," Amherst said.

Bolan pulled another DM-51 from his LBE strap. "This will help even the odds," Bolan said as he tossed the grenade.

BOLAN KEYED the microphone of his radio as they exited the warehouse. "Cooper to Lareza, come in."

No reply.

The Executioner gritted his teeth, wondering if something in this particular warehouse prevented communications. Earlier Lareza had mentioned his inability to raise Amherst on the radio, and that had been about the same time she was inside this building. They cleared the warehouse within a minute and skirted both buildings to come up on Lareza's side. Bolan crouched, the echo of police sirens very close now.

"Cooper to Lareza, do you read?"

Still nothing. Bolan ordered Amherst to head for the front gate and stall the arriving police units while he located Lareza. She started to protest, but the look he gave her said arguments wouldn't have been a good idea. She nodded, squeezed his forearm and then jumped to her feet and raced for the gate.

Bolan checked his surroundings and headed for Lareza's last known position, easily determined by the motionless form of the terrorist, lying still where he'd fallen. As he drew near the chain-link fence, Bolan could clearly make out the reason Lareza hadn't answered his radio. He lay motionless in a rapidly growing pool of blood. The Executioner used the snips in his utility tool to quickly cut an opening in the fence. He raced to Lareza's side. The cop lay with his head on a rock, some of the blood still oozing from his open throat. Bolan shook his head, whispered an ancient battlefield eulogy and then got to his feet.

Noise caused Bolan to turn in time to see a lone terrorist rush him, the murder weapon he'd used on Lareza still clutched in his bloody fist. Bolan sidestepped the blade as the terrorist slashed crazily, trying to cut open his belly. He delivered a knife-hand strike to his adversary's wrist while simultaneously grabbing the terrorist's collar. The knife flew from numbed fingers. Bolan delivered a foot sweep as he yanked backward and took the terrorist to his back. He directed a ridge hand to the guy's throat, crushing cartilage and rupturing blood vessels. The terrorist grabbed at his throat, and blood began to ooze from his mouth. He began to choke within seconds.

Bolan refused to stand there and wait for the terrorist to die. Other men might have derived some personal satisfaction from watching him suffer, but the Executioner wasn't like other men. He'd seen enough suffering to last a hundred lifetimes, maybe even a thousand. So in an undeserved act of mercy, Bolan drew his Beretta, pointed it at the terrorist's forehead and squeezed the trigger.

Bolan turned to see the cops had arrived. He was distant enough that he could slip away without being spotted. Amherst would, of course, find Lareza's body. There wasn't a thing he could do about that. When she saw the terrorist, she'd probably guess what had happened. When time permitted and it was right, he'd call her or see her personally and explain.

But even if he didn't—or it took him a little extra time—something told him she'd understand.

Mack Bolan had a hunch.

Police reports from the abandoned movie lot near Salton Lake made no mention of Hal Brognola's body. They had found a number of deceased men—some of whom Bolan bet were linked to Jemaah Islamiyah in one way or another—but no one even closely matching Brognola's description. They found the burned-out hulk of his car, but the CSI quickly confirmed the absence of human remains in the wreckage. That meant Hal Brognola was alive.

Bolan decided to play his hunch in true Executioner fashion. So it came as no surprise when he drove up the steps of Leonard Weste's estate in the car he commandeered from an inattentive chauffeur and crashed through the front doors.

The surprises kept coming when Weste's pair of bruiser bodyguards tried to take down Bolan with nothing more than brute force. Bolan dispatched both with his bare hands, hardly breaking stride.

In the last quarter of the Bolan blitz, judgment came for Leonard Weste and his criminal associates within the confines of those palatial estates. Once he'd cleared the bodyguards, Bolan encountered Hamzah and Santoso, who foolishly attempted to cut him down with machine pistols. The Executioner—a Beretta 93-R in one hand and the .44 Magnum Desert Eagle in the other—quickly took out those purveyors of death, once and for all.

But his final showdown with Sonny Tan and Jarot Pane offered Bolan the most satisfaction. The looks on their faces when they couldn't decide if they faced flesh and blood or a spirit returned from the grave made it almost worth all the hell he'd walked through. In the interest of completing the picture, though, Bolan made sure that he only wounded them. They would make excellent witnesses for Wikert and Starkey, who would only need their testimony to fill in the gaps.

When at last the Executioner faced Weste, he had already determined there wouldn't be any games. One way or another, whether or not he'd had anything to do with the fate of Harold Brognola, Weste would pay a heavy price.

"Let me put this in the simplest terms I know," Bolan told him, leveling the barrel of the Beretta, its muzzle still hot from having put a bullet in Jarot Pane's leg. "You tell me where the federal agent is, and I'll spare you twenty years in prison."

"You'll let me walk away?"

Bolan shrugged. "Whatever. It's no skin off my nose. I have no proof against you of any wrongdoing, other than the company you keep. And having friends isn't against any DEA law I know of. Just tell me where he is."

So Weste spilled it and the Executioner found his friend right where he'd been told, tied up in the basement wine cellar of Weste's estate. But what Bolan hadn't mentioned were the charges the FBI, BATF and Department of Homeland Security planned to file for aiding and abetting known fugitives of the law, consorting with individuals in terrorist organizations, bribery, blackmail, aiding in the kidnapping of a federal agent and coercion of public officials. All told, they carried a sentence of eighty-five years to life.

Leonard Weste would have a very long time to think on it.

Epilogue

Mack Bolan pushed through the door of Hal Brognola's secluded room at a small private hospital on the southern fringe of Beverly Hills.

The Stony Man chief looked up as he finished buttoning a brand-new shirt. Bolan watched as his friend swept a suit jacket off a nearby chair and gingerly shrugged into it. With the exception of a few minor cuts to his face, he looked no different than usual. He noticed the grimace in Brognola's face.

"Still hurting?"

As always, Brognola remained stoic. "I've got a bruise the size of Montana on my ass, so, yes, I'm still hurting."

Bolan chuckled. "Face it, Hal. Neither of us is getting younger."

"Speak for yourself," Brognola grumbled.

"So tell me again how exactly you managed to get through that alive?"

"I've already told you," Brognola deadpanned. "You're just ribbing me now."

"No, I'm really not sure. You were kind of delirious when I found you. Said something about falling down a hole?" Bolan smiled, unable to resist teasing the Stony Man chief a bit.

"I fell through rotted boards into a basement. I landed on my derriere and hit my head just hard enough to knock me out. I guess Santoso and Hamzah figured I'd be worth more to them alive than dead."

Bolan shook his head, and all trace of humor disappeared. "I know you're sure as hell more valuable to Stony Man alive than dead. Do me a favor next time, Hal."

"Anything."

"Stick to leading," Bolan said. "It's what you're best at. Leave all the heavy lifting to me. Got it?"

Brognola stared long at his friend and finally replied, "I know. So here ends the lesson."

Bolan delivered a short nod. "Now, let's get the hell out of here. I'll buy you breakfast."

"Actually, I need to get back. The Man's going to want a full report."

"Barb already filled him in."

"Aw, for crying out loud!"

"Relax, Hal," Bolan said. "Everything's back to normal. You don't have to worry about anymore talk of disbanding."

"Why's that?"

"Simple," the Executioner replied with grin, "Barb can be very persuasive when she wants to be."